The
Crystal
Tower
of
Light

The
Crystal
Tower
of
Light

Ríona
McGonagle

Illustrated by:
Sharon O'Grady

ARLEN
HOUSE

First published by Arlen House in January 2005

Arlen House
PO Box 222
Galway
Ireland
arlenhouse@ireland.com

ISBN   1-903631-34-3 paperback

Cover: Sharon O'Grady
Typesetting: Arlen House
Printed by: ColourBooks, Baldoyle, Dublin 13

CONTENTS

The
Crystal
Tower
of
Light

A
New
Beginning

1

Anna Shee had been running away from her past all of her life, so when she moved to the seaside village of BallyBoo with her two children, Luan and Seersha, she hoped that just this once her past wouldn't come back to haunt her. How wrong she was.

BallyBoo had always been a quiet peaceful village where nothing exciting ever happened. It was so very *unexciting* that the only way for the grown-ups to pass their time was to poke their noses into everybody else's equally *unexciting* business. The men fished and the women gossiped and every single day was exactly the same as the last.

That was until the arrival of the Shee family, of course. And then, all of a sudden, everything changed. Strange things began to happen, with no warning or explanation, and no two days were ever alike again. All sorts of strange rumours began to spread at the fishermen's wives' coffee mornings, to which Anna Shee was never invited, needless to say. The fishermen's wives had the same conversation every morning, adding in whatever disturbing new information they had gathered about Anna Shee over the last twenty-four hours.

"She's a witch and that's all there is to it", Mrs Biscuit remarked one morning, as she slobbered a cream cake all over her face. "How else could she heal old Mike Molloy with the very touch of her hand, when no doctor in the country could make him better?" she continued between mouthfuls. The other wives nodded in agreement.

"She can read the future in the stars too", Mrs Parker added. "I spotted her with my own two eyes through the window last night". The wives shook their heads in disgust.

"And to make matters worse", Mrs Biscuit butted in, wanting to be the centre of attention as always, "her husband must have run away and left her - I'd say he got sense in the end. Maybe she trapped him into marrying her with a love potion!"

Mrs Biscuit had a very active imagination for a human being but even she couldn't begin to imagine why Anna Shee appeared so very odd.

Even so much as a glimpse of Anna's fiery red hair, so long that it swept the ground behind her, was enough to stop every wife in her tracks. They would feel a shiver creeping down their spine, hitch up their skirts and dart off in the opposite direction as fast as their high heels would carry them.

"You all know that she's lowering the tone of our beautiful village, ladies! So how can we get rid of her from BallyBoo?" was all Mrs Biscuit really wanted to know, being the snob that she was.

"Why don't we burn her at the stake like people did with the witches in the Middle Ages?" Mrs Spark always piped up at this stage, her eyes gleaming excitedly at the very thought.

"Not a wise idea, Mrs Spark", Mrs Biscuit would reply, shaking her head sadly at her not-so-bright neighbour's idea, "the police would have us locked up in prison before we could even say 'BallyBoo!' if we did something like that. No, we'll just have to make her feel so unwelcome here that she will pack her bags and go back to whatever strange place she came from in the first place. That's the only way to get rid of her". And that's exactly what they intended to do.

Sometimes Anna Shee would watch the fishermen's wives through the little window in her cozy cottage by the sea. She longed that just one of them would let her be their friend. But that wasn't very likely to happen. She had tried her best to fit in - to be the same as everyone else but no matter how hard she tried people were still afraid of her because she wasn't the same as them.

What was it about her they were so afraid of, she wondered? Was it the fact that she was a single mother now that her dearly loved husband had been taken away from her against his will? Was it her red ankle-length hair?

She knew that the fishermen of BallyBoo were terribly superstitious when it came to red haired women. Whenever they caught a glimpse of a red haired woman before setting sail (more often than not Anna Shee herself), they decided there and then that the bad luck and evil magic she brought to them would make them drown at sea that very morning. So they would turn around and head straight for home again. They were almost as silly as their wives in that regard. But not quite. Anna knew perfectly well that her red hair didn't really bring bad luck *or* evil magic with it, but then she understood the basis of *real* magic, unlike the human population of BallyBoo.

Anyway, Anna decided that maybe it didn't matter too much that the fishermen and their wives didn't like her. They clearly weren't nice people, and who wants to make friends with people who aren't nice! And besides, she had a great friend in her son Luan. She could always talk to him, but he was only an eleven-year-old boy, and he just wasn't old enough to understand everything yet. The only thing he was interested in was football, football and more football. And then there was baby Seersha, but she was so tiny that she couldn't even speak properly yet, never mind understand a grown-up conversation!

Anna wished her husband was still with her, but he had disappeared into thin air the last time her past had caught up with her. Still, she was lucky to have Luan to help her. He was taking his role as 'man of the house' very seriously since his father vanished, or so she liked to believe! But boys are boys and they can't become responsible grown-ups overnight, and Luan was no exception!

So she filled her days doing all the mother's work and all the father's work, becoming the first fisherwoman BallyBoo had ever seen.

"My mum says your mum is a *witch*!" Luan was used to hearing from his classmates whenever he scored a goal against one of them.

"No she's not! She's actually the best all-in-one mother and father in the whole world, if you must know what she is!" Luan always retorted quickly. That was the best way of shutting them up! And he was right about his mum being the best in the world, he wouldn't swop her for anything, although nothing could ever replace his daddy.

The truth about Anna Shee, before we go any further, was that she was an ex-fairy princess. Unfortunately for her, that didn't mean that she could change all of her fairy habits and ways in the blink of an eye, no matter how much she wanted to fit in with the fishermen's wives of BallyBoo. And no matter where Anna was running from, or running to, she always stayed by the seaside. She would gaze absently out to sea, day after day, looking much further than the human eye could see, even with the best pair of binoculars ever invented.

She would gaze deep into the Atlantic Ocean, somewhere between the west coast of Ireland and America, where she could just about make out the misty coastline of her motherland. Home. *Teernoman*, as the fairies called it in their ancient Gaelic language. The land of eternal life. Anna Shee was homesick every time the word 'Teernoman' rolled off the tip of her tongue. But she could never return home.

Now Teernoman had a funny habit of changing location from time to time. Sometimes it would sail southward towards the Mediterranean Sea if the fairies wanted to top up their tan, or up towards the North Pole for a bit of ice-skating or sleigh-riding, but mostly it stayed in the same place where the sun was always shining, but where it wasn't *too* hot and it wasn't *too* cold. But then, although we humans might find the idea of an island being able to sail to wherever it pleases a bit strange, it was a perfectly normal thing in Teernoman. After all, we have to remember that when we're dealing with fairies, everything is possible!

There were no fairy men in Anna's motherland. Just fairy women. Women builders, women army chiefs, women coal miners, with not a man in sight. Unless of course you include the brave human explorers like Anna's husband who landed there by accident and were captured and treated as slaves.

Such human men were bound to the chains of eternal slavery and were under the control of the ferocious Queen Danu the Great, ruler of the land, who just happened to be Anna's mother. Luan called Queen Danu 'nasty Grandma' when he was little because his human grandma was so nice, the exact opposite of Anna's mother in fact.

When Luan was a little boy and demanded a bedtime story, Anna would tell him about the first time she laid eyes on his dad. No matter how many times she told him the same story, he wanted to hear it again and again. It was so magical and scary and enthralling for a little boy who had never experienced the wonders of Teernoman for himself.

"Once upon a time", she would begin, just like any other fairy tale, as she tucked him into bed, "long before you were born, your daddy was a wonderful explorer who travelled the fierce and dangerous seas of the world. One day, he landed on the misty, magical shore of Teernoman, quite by accident, after a terrible storm. An evil spy scanning the land for intruders found him washed ashore, along with the wreckage of his ship, all cut and bleeding. She (for the evil spy was of course a woman) brought him straight to nasty Grandma's crystal fairy fort".

"Does nasty Grandma *really* have a crystal fairy fort?" Luan would pipe up, a sudden sparkle in his eye at the very thought of it. "Indeed she does, my dear. It's surrounded by huge smoking volcanoes for protection and every single thing inside the fort is made from crystal - her throne, the cobblestones in the courtyard, even the trees and toys; it's a beautiful place. And what's more, in the middle of nasty Grandma's fairy fort, stands the Crystal Tower of Light. It's the most breathtaking thing I have ever seen, and *I've* seen a lot of things!"

"Can we go there someday, mum, even if it's only for a holiday?"

"We'll see, maybe if things change", Anna would sigh sadly. "Now, back to my story".

"Daddy was dragged along the ground the whole way to the fairy fort where nasty Grandma was sitting on her throne waiting for him, and I was by her side. Your daddy was in terrible pain by the time he arrived, and his poor skin was torn to shreds but his sense of humour hadn't been the slightest bit damaged. He took one look at nasty Grandma and then at me, and do you know what he did?"

"What, mum?"

"He started to sing".

"What did he sing?"

"This queen that I see is an ugly cow,
Alas for me, to her I must bow.
The beauty beside her has stolen my heart,
Whip me and lash me but from her I won't part!

'*Silence! Silence! Shut the human up! To the dungeons vith him!!!*' roared nasty Grandma to her guards, turning purple in the face with rage. It was very funny. I had to hide my laughter before nasty Grandma saw me!

"I had never even seen a real human before, let alone hear one sing. I used to colour them in in my colouring books when I was small, just like you colour in pictures of fairies in your colouring books, but I never thought that they *really* existed. I thought they were just made up".

"Am I a human or a fairy, mum? I mean, if you're a fairy and daddy's a human, then what am I?" Luan asked, looking confused.

"You, my dear, are a handsome human boy just like your daddy. But Seersha is a fairy like me. Boys are the same as their fathers and girls are the same as their mothers, see? That's why we have to be careful that nasty Grandma doesn't steal Seersha, because nasty Grandma knows that when Seersha gets a bit bigger, she will have fairy powers just as magical as hers and mine. I'm afraid that if nasty Grandma were to get her hands on little Seersha, she would try to make her as nasty as herself!"

That seemed to satisfy Luan's curiosity for a while. He was growing too sleepy to ask complicated questions at any rate. Anna continued her story.

"'Don't you dare even think about visiting that human beast in the dungeons!' nasty Grandma snapped at me, when she saw me smiling at him as he was being dragged away. Of course, I was just the same as every other young and curious fairy or human. When their mother tells them *not* to do something, well then of course they're going to do what they're not supposed to!

"You know that black beauty spot under your eye Luan?" Anna asked, touching the big black freckle she was talking about.

"But I thought that was just a big freckle?" Luan always replied.

"Nope, it's definitely a beauty spot, my dear".

"The boys at school say it looks girly", he answered, yawning.

"They don't know very much then", said Anna. "That beauty spot is the very same as your father had, and it has a magic power over the fairies. Every fairy woman who sees a human with a spot like that one below your eye feels a bolt of lightning go through her heart and falls instantly in love with him. It can be a very dangerous thing".

"Is that how you fell in love with dad?" Luan inquired.

"That was exactly how I fell in love with dad. Every night I would creep out of bed and tiptoe past nasty Grandma's room as she lay in her smelly mud bubble bath to make her beautiful. I'd steal mountains of food from the banqueting hall when nobody was looking and pop open the secret dungeon door, jumping through it just before her night guards would catch a glimpse of me. Daddy and I would have a midnight feast together in his dungeon cell. The tasty food I brought him made a welcome change from the scraps and pond scum that daddy was given to eat and drink day after day. As soon as our midnight feast was over, and our tummies were full, he would compose a new poem for me".

Luan screwed up his face at the idea of drinking pond scum with tadpoles in it.

"I just hope that doesn't mean the tadpoles turned into big slimy green frogs in dad's tummy!" he mused aloud. He had a horrible image in his head of slimy frogs bulging from his dad's insides, trying to break out of his tummy and leaving a big hole in his skin after their escape.

"No, Luan!" she laughed, "thank goodness! Daddy had enough to worry about besides growing frogs in his tummy!"

That satisfied him for a moment, but then his curiosity got the better of him again.

"Hold on, mum, was the dungeon made out of crystal too?"

"Not a chance. Do you really think nasty Grandma liked her prisoners enough to let them live in a crystal dungeon? No way, Luan! The dungeon was smelly and rat-infested and as dark as dark can be. Anyway, do you want to hear the rest of my story?" Luan nodded.

"Right, where were we? Ah yes, Daddy would compose a new poem for me every single night. He would tell me wonderful tales of the human world. All about cars and planes and walking on the moon. We planned our escape together, slowly and carefully, and nothing in the whole world was going to stop us. I didn't dare tell anyone my secret in case nasty Grandma would hear it. She would have murdered me if she had known what I was up to, but luckily for me she was too busy murdering everybody else in Teernoman to notice me most of the time! Only on the very night of our great escape did I tell my huge secret to my best friend Cara Shee. I couldn't possibly have left without saying goodbye to *her*. She thought I had finally gone crazy, but she wished me luck and gave me *this* so that I would never forget her".

Anna took out what looked like a little shimmering golden locket from her pocket. It was swinging from a golden chain. She let it slide gently through her fingers. "The locket of remembrance", she whispered, holding it close to her heart.

At this stage Luan didn't even move his head to have a look at it. He had fallen fast asleep, dreaming peacefully about football no doubt, with not a care in the world. She would kiss him goodnight, switching off the bedroom light. He always seemed to fall fast asleep just before she managed to finish her story. Maybe it was all for the best, she thought, as she snuggled up in her own bed, drifting into a deep sleep herself.

An
Eerlish
Imposter

2

One fine day during the summer holidays, Anna had been up since early morning baking little Seersha's birthday cake. She was one year old today! The cake was a massive white chocolate fairy fort that looked just like nasty Grandma's fort. It even had a Crystal Tower of Light in the middle of it, made from lumps of sugar stacked up high, with a layer of fresh cream on top. It was the most beautiful cake ever seen.

"Mmm, yummy!" said Luan, swiping a big lump of cream with his finger as his mother's back was turned.

"I saw that, Luan Shee!" she laughed, "you know perfectly well that I've got eyes at the back of my head!"

"Now, I'm going to go catch some nice fish for Seersha's birthday dinner. Do you think you could look after her just for a little while? I promise I won't be long!" Anna asked Luan, as she turned around to face him.

"As long as I can have as many chips and as much cake as I want with my fish at dinner!" he replied, his mouth watering at the very thought of so much tasty food.

"It's a deal then!" said Anna, "but whatever you do, don't leave Seersha on her own!"

Anna sailed the seas, scanning the ocean for the biggest tastiest fish she could find. At last she was satisfied with her catch, and turned her little boat around in the direction of home.

She rowed contentedly across the rippling water, watching the world go by through the hazy sunshine. Seagulls were circling the coastline, diving into the water for a quick snack now and then and the fishermen were heading for home, proudly showing off their catch to all the passers-by. If only every day could be this peaceful, Anna thought, never ceasing to marvel at the true freedom of this human world.

Luan sat and played with his little sister for a while. But he soon got bored and she soon got tired. She was too little to play proper games like the big kids played. He looked out the window and saw his friends playing a game of football on the beach. They looked like they were having so much fun. Luan just *had* to join them, he couldn't stop himself. He knew his mum's last words as she left the cottage were that he was *never* to leave Seersha all on her own, but his mother was far away now, and she would *never* find out if he left Seersha alone just for a little while ...

All of a sudden Anna Shee heard a tremendous wailing sound in the distance. She woke up from her daze to see the entire population of BallyBoo banging their front doors behind them and running in the direction of ...

"My house!" Anna whispered, turning pale in fright. "What's going on?"

She dreaded to think.

Anna rowed home faster than anyone had ever rowed before, plunging her oars swiftly through the water. There was no time to waste. She leaped out of the boat as she approached the shore and raced home along the beach, her long hair sweeping the sand up in a cloud behind her.

She pushed and shoved her way through the nosey crowd trying to peer through the windows of her cottage to see what was happening.

"Luan, Luan, what's wrong?" Anna cried as she stumbled through the front door, falling flat on her face.

Luan didn't speak.

Standing still as a statue and guilty as can be, he raised a shaking arm into the air and stretched out his index finger.

Anna followed the direction in which his finger was pointing with her eyes. It was pointing at Seersha's cot. Anna breathed a sigh of relief.

"Oh Luan, silly me, I should have told you that baby Seersha is teething, and that makes her cry and wail more than usual!" she said, picking herself up from the floor and rubbing Luan's hair fondly.

"She'll be back to her cheerful self before you know it!"

But Luan's body still didn't move and neither did his lips.

"Look, Luan", Anna said trying to convince him by going over to Seersha's cot to pick her up. "Maybe she's hungry too!"

"Clap handssss for clever mammy, I AM sssstarving, haven't had a bite to eat in dayssss", came a deep crackling husky reply from inside Seersha's cot.

Anna could have sworn that she heard an old man's voice coming from the cot, but there was only Seersha in it, and she was still talking baby jibber-jabber that very morning. And besides, it wasn't possible for an old man to fit into a baby's cot - no man could be that small! She hoped she was only imagining things, but she peeped into Seersha's cot just to be certain.

Anna Shee jumped back the length of the room in fright, knocking Luan down behind her. Much to her horror, up popped a head. A head that was spitting and snarling at her.

It certainly looked like Seersha's face except ... "look at that wicked mouth of dirty crumbling teeth, mummy!" Luan shrieked, suddenly finding his voice. "That's not our baby Seersha! Look at its yellowy wrinkled skin! Look at its grey hair!"

At that point the baby imposter, who looked like a tiny withered old man, somersaulted out of the cot and all hell broke loose. It swooped from rafter to rafter of the roof as Anna did her best to grab it. It was roaring like a wild beast as it went.

It threw photo frames and vases to the ground, breaking them into little bits. It jumped on top of Seersha's beautiful birthday cake that Anna had spent so much time making, breaking it into little pieces and stamping it into the ground. It took a swipe at Anna's hair with a scissors, chopping it all off in one go. It even had the cheek to take a big bite out of the tail of Spike the dog, who had been sleeping peacefully in the corner of the room, far too old and deaf to heed the entire racket. He woke with an almighty jump and started whimpering, although more in shock than in pain.

Anna had had just about enough of this beastly imposter, her rage doubling and tripling by the second.

At last she managed to grab it by the neck, so tightly that there was no escaping from her.

"Pleasssse don't hurt me, mammy. Sssseersssssha's sssssorry. Sssseersssssha's a good girl, mammy", it hissed in the same old man's voice as before.

"You're right", said Anna sweetly, holding in her anger for a moment, "my Seersha is a very good little girl, BUT YOU'RE NOT MY SEERSHA! TELL ME WHAT YOU DID WITH HER, YOU BEAST!" she bellowed, shaking it like it had never been shaken before.

"Hah! You musssst be joking", it snarled, "I'll never tell you that. Top sssssecret information that isss! Rule number 1 in the Eerlissssh handbook - never tell who you're working for or elsssse nobody will employ you ever again".

Luan looked frantically from his mother to the beast, not knowing what was going on. All he knew was that Seersha had been stolen when he had gone out to play football with the boys and that his mother was going to murder him as soon as she found out that he had left her all alone! He could feel the beads of guilt-ridden sweat gathering on his brow and slowly beginning to trickle down his troubled face.

"An *Eerlish*, so *that's* what you are then", said Anna, knowing this was a clear sign that her past had caught up with her yet again. Her mother, Queen Danu the Great, would stop at nothing to ruin her daughter's life.

Anna knew perfectly well that the only place where Eerlishes existed was Teernoman. She had often heard of these Eerlish beasts being employed by rich fairies to replace human children that the fairies had stolen from their homes and families.

"Where's my Seersha?"

"I'm not telling you!" the Eerlish replied with a cheeky grin.

"Right, that's it!" said Anna. "I've had just about enough of your cheek. I think you could do with a nice cold SALTY bath in the sea, what do you say, *Eerlish?*"

The Eerlish's frightened eyes bulged out of its head so much that Anna hoped they might pop out altogether. That would serve it right.

Anna had never come across a real live Eerlish before and hoped she wouldn't come across one again, but she did learn one important fact about Eerlishes when she was at Child Army Camp in Teernoman (which is the fairy version of human schools, but a lot stricter) - probably the most important fact of all - that Eerlishes hated, detested even, *every* form of salt. It could be salt on a plate of chips or sea-salt, it made no difference which type. The very mention of the word drove them to madness and this scruffy little beast between Anna's hands was no exception.

Anna Shee flung the front door of her little cottage wide open, storming through the crowd, with the beast kicking and biting, snivelling, drivelling and dribbling slime onto her fingers all the way to the seashore.

Luan followed close behind, feeling guiltier by the minute.

She waded knee-deep into the sea, plunging the Eerlish into the water by the scruff of its dirty neck. The salty water began to gurgle and fizz up around it.

"Would you like to tell me now where my little Seersha is?" she said in a frightening tone of voice. "I'll set you free if you do".

"No way!" it hissed, trying to spit at Anna, but the spit landed "splat!" back on its own face.

She plunged it deeper and deeper, longer and longer, until the salt began to seep through its wrinkled leathery skin. The skin began to crackle and sizzle like a frying sausage in the salt and huge ugly sores appeared out of nowhere all over its surface, oozing thick yellow pus with the consistency of melted cheese. The Eerlish's scrawny body began to shrivel up like seaweed. Anna had to hold her breath with the stench of it.

"Alright, alright, I'll tell you, Anna Sssshee", the Eerlish spluttered, its will-power growing weak. "Qu-qu-qu", it whispered in exhaustion.

"Come on, spit it out, I don't have time for games", Anna commanded unsympathetically.

"Qu-queen Danu the Great'ssss fort", it blurted out.

That was all Anna needed to know.

True to her word, she set the Eerlish free, and watched the pathetic creature scurry frantically towards the sand dunes along the shore, spluttering and gasping for breath all the way. It glanced back every few seconds to make sure she wouldn't pounce on it again. There was no way it was going to survive in the salty human world. It would die the long painful and miserable death that it deserved for committing such a terrible crime as stealing an innocent little baby. Anna watched it for a while longer, until it was finally swallowed up by a hungry sand hole.

"Good riddance to bad rubbish", she thought. Anna waded slowly back to shore, with Luan by her side. She was not looking forward to the neighbours' reaction.

It might have been difficult to try to make friends before the Eerlish's visit, but now it was going to be impossible. Still, she had more important things on her mind now, like rescuing baby

Seersha from the harsh hands of Queen Danu the Great, before it was too late. Queen Danu had gone one step too far in stealing her granddaughter from Anna, and Anna was going to have to make sure nothing like that would ever happen again.

The neighbours had covered their noses with scarves to avoid the stench of the Eerlish's rotting skin, which had wafted ashore by now.

The entire Parker family's eyes were bulging out of their sockets on witnessing such strange events.

"Alright, the show is over, nosey-parkers", she called out to them, as they stood rooted to the spot staring at her. "I hope you enjoyed it!"

The women would certainly have a great topic of conversation for their coffee mornings for years and years to come.

Anna strode boldly past them all, marching Luan straight home. She knew exactly what had to be done to save her precious little Seersha, and save her she most certainly would.

Hatching
a
Plan

3

Luan lay awake all night, wondering what had become of little Seersha. He couldn't help but think that Seersha would be tucked up fast asleep in her cot in the next room if he had done what his mother had asked him to do, and looked after her.

He dare not tell Anna the truth, or she would ground him for life. If only there was something he could do to make everything go back to normal again ...

Anna sat on the lonely beach, casting her eyes towards the stars glittering in the night sky. Everything seemed so peaceful now that it was hard to believe the amount of chaos the Eerlish imposter had created only a few hours earlier.

She picked a bright star out of the sky, and with great concentration she began to draw it closer to her. It moved slowly at first, barely noticeable, then it shot through the darkness like a cannonball, landing in Anna's lap.

It was a big star, with a smooth golden surface, perfect for writing a message on. Anna blew all the stardust off it and began to write. She sensed a shadow creeping up behind her.

"Oh, Luan, don't scare me like that! I nearly jumped out of my skin just now!" she said as Luan sat down beside her.

"I couldn't sleep, so I brought you what's left of Seersha's birthday cake", he said, handing her a plate with a heap of squashed creamy crumbs on it.

"Thanks, Luan, I couldn't sleep either", she replied, rubbing his hair fondly.

"What are you doing, mum?" Luan inquired, suddenly noticing the smooth golden star stretched out in front of her.

"I'm sending a starletter to Teernoman. The fairies don't need postmen to deliver their letters. We just capture a star in the night sky and tame it just like humans tame animals".

"Like Spike the dog?" inquired Luan.

"Exactly", Anna replied. "Then we write a message on the star and send it to our friends. It's quite simple to do once you know how. Every shooting star you see in the sky is really just a message being sent between old friends in Teernoman and our world".

"Can I send a shooting star?" Luan asked in excitement, forgetting all about Seersha for a split second.

"Not tonight, dear, but some other time I'll teach you".

With that, Anna picked up the star, spun herself round and round in circles to gather speed and flung it like a frisbee high into the night sky. They watched it shoot over the moon, until finally it disappeared into the darkness.

"That letter was to my old friend Cara Shee, Luan. Tomorrow morning I'm going to have to leave you at nice Grandma's house for a few days while I go to rescue little Seersha from nasty Grandma's fairy fort", Anna told him.

Luan's face suddenly dropped.

"Why can't I come with you?" he pleaded.

"Teernoman is far too dangerous for an ordinary human boy, never mind a boy with a beauty spot", Anna replied, "and besides, I have to take the boat there and you know how seasick you get in the boat!"

Luan grimaced at the very thought of being seasick.

"Now, off to bed with you, my dear, I have lots of work to do before I set sail".

Anna stayed up all night in her cottage, drawing up maps of her homeland to the best of her memory, which was becoming a little bit fuzzy to say the very least.

An incoming star lit up the night sky far above BallyBoo as it 'swooshed' through the cold air, landing on her doorstep.

"Just as well the neighbours didn't see that too or they'd have the police after me!" she said to herself out loud.

She picked up the star, and dusted it until she could make sense of its message. She read it aloud:

"Anna Shee, my dearest friend,
Your story it saddens me,
Together we'll plan Danu's end,
And rescue Seersha Shee.

Tomorrow night the moon will be bright,
The fairies will feast in glee,
That is your chance to better your plight,
Sail home, and help us be free".

Anna traced her fingers over the name at the bottom of the message. 'Cara Shee', still the same as ever!

It was so good to hear from her best friend after so long, and it was nice to have someone she could rely on for a change.

"Tomorrow night the moon will be bright,

The fairies will feast in glee", she read aloud again.

That could only mean one thing - the Feast of the Full Moon.

Anna remembered the Feast of the Full Moon from her childhood. Every single day she would daydream about it as she learned her lessons in Child Army Camp. It was the only good idea her mother had ever had and it was the biggest event in the fairy calendar. Even bigger than Christmas and Hallowe'en and Thanksgiving put together.

Every time there was a full moon, each and every fairy in the land would make a long and dangerous and tiring pilgrimage to the renowned Crystal Tower of Light in Queen Danu the Great's fort.

The Crystal Tower of Light could be seen for miles around, rising higher into the sky than the volcanoes around it. She recalled how the light of the moon bounced off it and made it more dazzling than ever as it shimmered through the darkness.

Queen Danu the Great would emerge from the top of the tower in her golden silk cloak and open the festivities with the flick of her ceremonial magic wand.

Fireworks would burst through the sky, followed by showers of gifts falling out of the heavens, keeping the fairy children out of mischief while their mothers ate and drank and sang and danced non-stop for three whole days and three whole nights.

It was the best party ever, and it was also the best time ever to sneak into Teernoman, as Anna knew well.

Only the dwarfs and animals and slaves weren't invited and they weren't half as dangerous or clever as an evil fairy, or so she hoped!

"Right, I'd better try to get some sleep before I set off in the morning, or I'll be too tired to rescue Seersha and free the fairies from my mother's harsh rule", she said to herself, before finally dozing off in her rocking chair.

Time was ticking by ever so slowly for Luan as he lay stretched out on his bed, staring blankly at the ceiling. He was feeling guiltier and guiltier, and was afraid that his head might burst with the guilt if he didn't do something soon. Nice Grandma was very nice, but he didn't want to let his mum go to Teernoman, just in case she would be captured by nasty Grandma and he would never see her again.

And besides, he was the man of the house now, and it was time for him to act like a man, and if that meant having to venture into the wilds of Teernoman and getting seasick in the process, well so be it!

There was only one thing for him to do.

Luan waited, listening to Anna rocking gently forwards and backwards in her chair. He waited for what seemed like hours and hours for her to fall sound asleep. At last he could hear her snoring gently.

Up he jumped in his pyjamas, tiptoeing into the sitting room. He had no time to waste.

As he grew accustomed to the darkness surrounding him, he spotted the maps of Teernoman that his mother had made. Luan silently gathered them as they lay on her sleepy lap, and he stole a basket of fruit from the kitchen.

The corner of his eye caught his mother's locket of remembrance shining like a little ball of fire through the darkness. He didn't really know what it was, but he wanted something for good luck, so he stuck it in his pocket as he sneaked through the front door.

The door creaked a little behind him. Anna stirred in her sleep, but not enough to realize what was going on.

Luan raced down to the harbour where his mother's little boat was moored, leaving a trail of fallen fruit behind him.

Off he set, plunging the little boat into the vast ocean, rowing urgently through the thick early morning fog. He was going to bring Seersha home to her mother. How happy she would be!

And then he would be able to tell Seersha bedtime stories too, all about his own adventures in Teernoman!

A
Voyage
Through
Darkness

4

Anna woke up with a jump. Dawn was breaking, and she had no time at all to waste. She was glad to see that all of her hair had grown back already, even though the Eerlish had chopped it off less than a day ago.

She had a good feeling about this new day.

"Luan, time to wake up, we've got a big day ahead of us!" she called, peeping her head around his bedroom door. But there was no sign of him.

"That's odd", she thought, "maybe he's gone sleepwalking again". Anna spotted an apple on the floor beside her and picked it up to put it back into the fruit basket. But the fruit basket had disappeared and so had her maps. She began to worry.

She spotted another apple beside the front door and bent over to pick it up. She opened the door to let in the fresh morning air, chilly as it was. "There's a pear on the path, *and* a peach, *and* a plum", she said, following the line of fruit right down to the little harbour where she kept her boat.

"Oh no", she groaned, looking aghast, "my boat's gone and Luan's gone and my fruit basket's gone and my maps are gone. He must have gone to Teernoman all alone to try to save little Seersha. The fairies will rip him to shreds. What can I do? I've no boat and I couldn't possibly steal one. And there's no other way for me to return to Teernoman. I'll never see my children again", Anna sobbed, overcome by grief.

Meanwhile, Luan was as happy as can be, sailing across the vast Atlantic Ocean in his pyjamas.

He hadn't even got sick once! He only wished there was someone with him so that he could boast about it!

BallyBoo was growing smaller and smaller behind him, until it was no more than a tiny speck on the horizon.

The thick fog lifted high into the sky as the sun finally broke through, and Luan was left looking at the emptiness of the bright turquoise sea glistening in front of him.

The sharp taste of sea salt coated his lips and the waves sprayed ice-cold water all over him to welcome him into their company as he rowed deeper and deeper into the ocean. He thought long and hard, trying to remember all the stories his mother had told him about nasty Grandma and Teernoman ever since he was little. "*Everything is possible in Teernoman*", that was her favourite saying, along with "*you never know what's round the corner there*".

He would have to be very careful if he wanted to save Seersha and be the first human since his father to escape from Teernoman alive. Then there was the other problem that he wasn't *really* the best map-reader in the world and didn't *really* have *any* idea in which direction he was rowing.

Still, he was quite sure that everything would work out just fine in the end. "It always did in mum's fairy tales anyway", he said to the waves, trying to reassure himself.

The day flew by and night was falling fast. Every so often Luan caught a glimpse of the full moon peeping shyly through the shadowy clouds above him.

Occasionally a shooting star whooshed across the sky, another help call from his mother to Cara Shee, although Luan would never have guessed it. He just liked to watch them flash by. Maybe some day he would learn to tame the stars, just like he had helped his mum to tame Spike the dog. That way he could send messages to his friends. Now that would be pretty cool!

Suddenly, a pink light appeared out of nowhere, heading straight for Luan. It wasn't a star, as far as he could tell. Or a shooting star, or even a fallen star. It was more like a pink spotlight skimming over the surface of the ocean.

"I've never seen a light like that before!" said Luan, with no one but the waves and the stars and the moon to hear him. "It can't possibly be a fairy light", he decided, or hoped, more like it! "I couldn't possibly be anywhere near Teernoman yet!" but he ducked for cover just in case he was wrong.

Whoever or whatever was shining the light must have heard him talking to himself out loud, because all of a sudden the pink light swung in his direction, landing right on him. It was no use trying to hide from it. The light made his insides tingle and tickle and he couldn't stop himself from rolling around the boat, laughing like a madman.

He looked down, expecting his pyjamas to have turned a girly pink colour.

"Aaaaaaaah!" he screamed, too shocked to laugh anymore.

"I can see my bones - and - and my heart - and - and is that the plum I've just eaten sliding down into my tummy?!"

Luan hopped and ducked all over the boat, rocking it from side to side as he tried his best to dodge the pink rays of the light, but it followed him round like a hunter about to pounce on its prey. Much to his horror, the stronger and closer the light got, the more of his insides he could see.

He had to do something to save himself - and quick.

What would people say if they knew he had failed in his mission before he even made it to Teernoman? He would never be able to live that down!

He grabbed the near-empty fruit basket from the deck and started to fire its contents in the direction of the light, one straight after the other, with all his strength. Apples and oranges were the only weapons he had thought of bringing with him.

"How stupid I am to have forgotten something as important as weapons!" he thought regretfully.

Luan thought he heard a thud, and then he was sure that he heard a thud, as the pink light suddenly disappeared into thin air.

"What a lucky escape", he said, as he lay down exhausted on the deck. The strength of the light had zapped his body of all its energy.

And then it began.

"Oooouuuuucch! Oooouuuuucch!"

A screeching wail that stretched for miles and miles and rippled the calm surface of the sea. Luan listened carefully. Even Seersha didn't wail as loud as that, and she definitely had a strong pair of lungs.

On and on it continued. He could have sworn that it was coming from the same direction as the pink light. There was only one thing for it. He would have to put a stop to it before the fairies heard it too. They would be sure to send out a sea-hunter to investigate the noise and the sea-hunter was bound to find him as well!

He tried to make out the shape of the shadow just in front of his mother's boat, where all the noise was coming from.

"I wonder what that could be? It could be a boat, but I've never seen a roundy-shaped boat before", he said, scratching his head with a puzzled expression as he studied the vessel in front of him. He would soon find out.

"Ahoy there, matie!" he called out, putting on his best pirate voice, just in case he was dealing with pirates. He tied up his boat and hopped onto the roundy one, without thinking.

"Ahoy, ahoy, how dare you 'ahoy me, matie!'" came a thundering reply to Luan's friendly greeting, along with a stinging smack across his face.

"Why, you almost knocked me stone dead with your flying fruit you, you ... beautiful boy!"

Luan rubbed his eyes in shock, not realising that he was drawing attention to his face. His beauty spot was on full view for this sailor woman to see, just as she finished her sentence.

A bolt of lightning pierced her heart, the very same bolt of lightning that Anna had felt when she first laid eyes on Luan's father a long time ago.

The sailor woman's voice suddenly changed, becoming sweet and cheerful. "But never mind about *me*, my dear, tell me about *you*", she said with a dazzling big smile.

She had already decided that nothing in the whole world was going to stop her from making this human boy her husband as soon as he was old enough, whether he liked it or not.

"I'm Dwaireen Dwairy, and it's a pleasure to meet you", she said, batting her lashless eyelids at the poor boy.

Luan gasped. The funniest looking woman, or sort-of-woman he had ever seen, was staring him in the face. She certainly looked nothing like his mother, that's for sure!

She would have been tiny if it weren't for the pink high heels she was wearing, heels so very, very high that they were as tall as she was, if not even taller. And that was just for starters.

Her face was as hairy as the fishermen's in BallyBoo, and if it weren't for the bright pink lipstick smeared all over her lips, and her matching pink sunglasses, he might have mistaken her for a man.

Luan's head was bursting with questions, the first springing to mind being why on earth she was wearing sunglasses in the middle of the night (or maybe they were moonglasses he thought, that would make a lot more sense). 'Dwaireen Dwairy', as she called herself, was only too happy to answer his questions.

"It goes like this, my lovely Mr Luan", she explained in a matter-of-fact tone of voice.

"I've been a dwairy all my life, the tallest dwairy in the world I might add", she said proudly.

Luan nearly choked with laughter.

"You! Tall! Your heels are taller than you are!" Dwaireen looked insulted.

"I take it you have *never* seen a dwairy before, have you?" she snapped. She seemed to change her mood every second.

"No, I suppose I haven't then", Luan replied, taken aback by her rudeness.

"A dwairy is a dwarf fairy", she continued.

"Does that mean I'm close to Teernoman?" Luan butted in, eager to find little Seersha.

"Ssssh, let me finish my story", replied Dwaireen in a huff.

"I've served the fairies my whole life. I've scrubbed their toilets and cooked their dinners and I am sick and tired of being treated like, like, like ..."

Luan was fed up with her whining already.

"That's all very interesting", he butted in, trying to keep on her good side, "but why are you wearing sunglasses and sailing alone at night?"

"I'm diamond hunting of course!" she exclaimed, as if it was the most normal thing in the world to be doing all alone at sea in the middle of the night. "And I'm going to be so stinking rich by the time the fairies return home from the Feast of the Full Moon that *they*'ll be the ones scrubbing *my* toilet for ever more".

"You can't possibly believe that you'll find diamonds in the sea!" Luan scoffed at such a ridiculous idea.

"Well where do you think they come from then?" Dwaireen asked, amazed at the boy's ignorance.

Luan shrugged his shoulders. He didn't know.

"Of course they come from the sea, they come from the mouth of a fish". Luan looked at her in disbelief.

"I'll show you if you don't believe me", she said, determined to prove her point.

With that, she put on her pink sunglasses, flicking on the pink light that Luan recognized so well and started to scan the seabed. She stretched a surprisingly long hand overboard, and hauled a big pink-scaled fish into the boat.

"See?"

She stuck her finger into its mouth to show Luan that she was right about the diamond teeth and that he was most certainly wrong. The clever fish smelt the dwairy flesh right in front of it and snapped its mouth shut, trapping her finger inside. She started to wail her familiar wail again.

"Oooouuuuucch!"

But she *was* telling the truth.

There, right before Luan's eyes, were two perfect rows of sparkling diamond teeth, more perfect than any diamond he had ever seen. Luan grabbed the fish, squeezing it tightly by its middle until it opened its mouth to let Dwaireen Dwairy retrieve her swollen finger with deep diamond tooth imprints on it.

She continued her explanation, forgetting all about her sore finger. "And these 'sunglasses' as you call them, are my very own fish x-ray system. I can see through the fish with them to see which ones still have their diamond teeth intact and which don't. Cost me a fortune these glasses did", she announced, "but they're the best diamond hunting tool on the market", she added, "and they'll x-ray just about anything!"

With that, she flicked them on at Luan just for fun. "Stop it! Stop it!" he laughed, feeling all tickly again.

"Time for some dinner", she announced, suddenly changing the subject and leading Luan down into her round shaped cabin below deck. Dwaireen produced a plate of steaming hot seafood stew and chewy octopus-leg spagetti for the hungry traveller. Its delicious aroma wafted up through his nostrils. How could he possibly refuse, especially since he hadn't got to eat his fish and chips and cake for Seersha's birthday the day before?

Luan licked his lips and tucked in. He ate and ate until he was stuffed like a pig. Although he may have been less enthusiastic if he had known what he was eating!

Little did the human boy know that the Dwairy family were known in Teernoman as the best cooks throughout the land, and nobody could possibly resist the smell of their succulent mouth-watering cooking. But that wasn't necessarily a good thing...

With a full belly and a feeling of warmth and coziness deep inside him, Luan Shee fell fast asleep, forgetting everything he had ever known.

Teernoman

5

While Luan Shee lay fast asleep on Dwaireen Dwairy's round boat, without a care in the world, Dwaireen decided to head for home. She had gathered enough diamonds to make her the richest Dwairy in Teernoman, as well as being the tallest one. She now had everything she had ever dreamed of in life within the grasp of her fingertips, and she was a very excited sort-of-woman!

For her seafood stew she had used the old magic recipe, with its secret ingredient, that had existed in the Dwairy family for generations, a magic recipe so powerful that it made its victim fall into a deep sleep and forget about his past.

Dwaireen, just like every other dwairy, was a greedy and sly creature by nature, and had already concocted a cunning little plan to keep Luan all for herself. But, fortunately for Luan, her plan went very, very wrong.

Dwaireen Dwairy was giddy with excitement after her successful night of fishing, so giddy that she completely forgot to switch off her x-ray diamond hunting glasses as she headed for home.

She switched on the engine of her boat.

It began to chug a little, then it started to spin around and around in circles like a spinning top, until it finally took off in the direction of Teernoman.

If a human eye had seen it, the human would have thought it was a whirlwind, it was going so fast and causing so much sea spray to fizz up around it. It was just as well that Luan was asleep or he really would have gotten sick this time, if not from the sea, then certainly from the dizziness!

She whirled carelessly through the crystal gates at the eastern port of Teernoman, with her pink light on at full blast and humming away happily to herself. The light bounced off the crystal gates, turning the night sky bright pink.

"Uh-oh", she thought to herself, but it was too late.

The fairies might have been busy partying to their heart's content at the Feast of the Full Moon, but they weren't foolish enough to leave the misty, rugged coastline of Teernoman unattended for anyone to sneak into their fair land. Queen Danu the Great would never be foolish enough to let anyone enter without her permission, especially a human boy with a beauty spot!

A shrill siren echoed all over the still night sky, signalling the arrival of an intruder.

In a split second, before Dwaireen had time to react, dozens of crystal boats had surrounded her vessel. There was no chance of escape. More dwairy police than she could possibly count jumped onto her boat, finding all her diamonds stashed away and Luan, the human, stretched out fast asleep in the cabin below.

The chief of police, wearing black high-heels like Dwaireen's, handcuffed her, despite her pleadings of innocence.

"I swear I didn't know what was on the boat, it's the human's fault, he was the one who kidnapped me when I was having a late night swim in the sea!" she said, sobbing big crocodile tears.

The chief of police knew better than to believe her.

"You are aware, Dwaireen Dwairy", the chief began, sounding very important, "that unauthorised diamond extraction in itself is a very serious crime?"

Dwaireen nodded without lifting her head. She was so ashamed of herself, not for her crime, but for getting caught.

"But aiding and abetting the importation of a filthy rotten smelly human into our lovely land is breaking every single law ever drawn up by our courts!" the chief of police boomed. (Of course, if the chief or any of her police force had noticed Luan's beauty spot, they wouldn't have been calling him a filthy rotten human at all - quite the opposite in fact!)

Dwaireen didn't understand all the big words the chief of police was churning out, but she understood enough to know she was going to be severely punished for her crimes.

"I hereby sentence you to appear before Queen Danu the Great. She shall choose a suitable punishment for you and your human friend!"

"No! Not Queen Danu! Anything but Queen Danu!" Dwaireen cried hysterically, her voice shaking at the very thought. "Please, I beg you, anything, anything else!"

The chief began to feel sorry for the pathetic creature handcuffed in front of her.

"Hmm, very well, seeing as this is your first offence. Let's start again shall we? Dwaireen Dwairy, I hereby sentence you and your human friend to be bound to the chains of eternal slavery by auction! Good day, Ma'am!"

With that the chief hopped back onto her own boat and sped away, leaving the whimpering criminal in the care of her orange-heeled police force.

Dwaireen and Luan were led ashore by their police escort and were locked up in tiny cages in preparation for their punishment of being bound to the chains of eternal slavery by auction.

It was just as well that Luan had slept through all the commotion or he would have found himself receiving a rather cold and nasty welcome to Teernoman, just as nasty a welcome as his father had received long before him.

As it happened, when Luan awoke, he felt refreshed and full of energy after his long deep sleep.

He could hear all kinds of strange exotic music around him but he couldn't see a single thing. Everything around him was pitch black.

It was just as well that he could hear perfectly well under the circumstances; maybe that would give him a clue as to where he was.

He could hear a loud drum-roll, then an orchestra of magical flute music, followed by a funny chant and hollow drum beat, that went something like 'Dina Dayna Dina Dayna', over and over again, getting higher and louder every time it was repeated. Little did he know that what the dwairies were chanting was 'Human being! Human being!' in their ancient Gaelic language. Many of them had never seen a real human being before and were very excited about his arrival in Teernoman. Luan felt like joining in, but he couldn't speak the language, or could he?

He couldn't remember if he could or not. In fact he couldn't remember very much at all.

Who was he?

Where was he?

And why on earth was he wearing pyjamas?!

Luan stood up, banging his head off something. He tried to stretch his arms and legs but he banged them off something too. He felt his way around him.

"What am I doing in a monkey cage, I couldn't possibly be a monkey, could I?" he wondered, having decided that he was trapped inside a moving monkey cage with thick iron bars.

Four strong dwairies were carrying the cage on their shoulders. Wearing orange high heels at the same time didn't seem to cause them the slightest bit of difficulty! And the monkey cage seemed to be covered over with black curtains on all sides. Luan was very confused. He could see a thin ray of sunlight just about penetrating a tiny slit in one side of the curtain. He peeked out through it.

Luan's cage was the centre of attention in a colourful parade making its way through a beach marketplace. Dwaireen was wasting her energy screaming and wailing in her cage close behind, but the chatter and clatter, hustle and bustle of the marketplace drowned her efforts out. They were being brought to the auction of eternal slavery.

Luan was shocked to see the funny looking creatures lining the beach as he passed them by.

He could see sows and does and ewes all queuing up at a beauty stall, waiting to get their skin dyed (just like humans get their hair dyed).

At another stall, Luan could see a dwairy artist painting butterfly wings under a huge magnifying glass. She had a different brush in each hand, each foot and in her mouth, and was busy splashing paint on all the passers-by too!

Everybody seemed to be paying for their purchases with diamonds. "So *that's* what people use to buy things", thought Luan. "It's strange that I didn't remember something as simple as what sort of money we use!"

There were stalls selling everything imaginable and even everything unimaginable under the sun.

Luan had a bird's eye view of the entire beach from his perch above everyone else.

Beyond the marketplace he could see a ridiculous looking dwairy sumo-wrestling competition. The two wrestlers were as wide as they were tall, and even *they* were wearing high heels. Their fans cheered and clapped and hissed and booed, not daring to take their eyes off their champions in case they would miss something.

Luan watched until a sand storm blew up around them, hiding them from his sight. He reckoned the easiest way of winning the fight would be to grab the opponent's high heel and trip them up so that they'd fall flat on their face.

"But then again, what would I know?" sighed Luan, suddenly feeling very lonely.

With a loud thud, Luan's monkey cage was dropped down onto a broad ledge of rock overlooking the marketplace. Still peeking through the slit in the black curtain, he noticed a black-heeled dwairy ringing a little bell in her hand.

Luan decided that whatever colour heels the women were wearing must be a sign of how important they were, black being the most important of all.

He watched the goings-on with fascination.

A row of monkey cages just like his own was stretched out in front of him.

The black-heeled dwairy rang her bell once more.

Absolutely every creature on the beach, sumo-wrestlers and all, dropped what they were doing and raced straight towards the black-heeled dwairy.

"Fair dwairies and animals of Teernoman", she called aloud, waiting for the noise and clapping to die down.

"Teernoman, so *that's* where I am", thought Luan. "That name does sound familiar, but I've no idea why".

The dwairy continued.

"Today we are free. Free from our chores, our cleaning, our washing, and our endless scrubbing for our ungrateful fairy mistresses. Today, we shall celebrate the Feast of the Full Moon in our own style. Today, my friends, it is *our* turn to be the mistresses!"

A great cheer arose from the crowd.

"Today, I welcome you all to the auction of eternal slavery, where the highest diamond bidder can have her choice of exotic slaves to serve her for all eternity. Let the auction begin!"

With that, the black curtains covering every cage were stripped off. The prisoners were just as shocked to see the sea of brightly coloured faces in front of them as the crowd of dwairies was to see the funny looking prisoners staring out from the cages.

The crowd let out a deafening roar on seeing Luan, gasping and 'oohing' and 'aahing' at this exotic creature.

"Must be a human", he overheard one dwairy say to another. "Just look at his ears, they *are ears*, aren't they?"

"Well, if they are, they're the silliest looking ears I've ever seen!" came the reply from her friend.

One by one, the miserable looking prisoners were sold. There was one dwairy amongst them, whom the black-heeled lady called 'Dwaireen', and Luan could have sworn that he had seen her somewhere before, but he couldn't for the life of him remember where.

He felt particularly sorry for a sulky woolly pig that was led away in chains by a hideous hag in a black cloak. He hoped that his new mistress would look a little bit friendlier.

At last it was his turn to be sold.

"Now for the moment you've all been waiting for".

The crowd hushed in anticipation. Luan could hear himself gulp aloud in fright.

"Ladies, I beg you to control yourselves, for I have here a fine specimen of a very rare breed indeed. No, ladies, your eyes do not deceive you, I have here a very much sought after human", the black-heeled lady said, poking him in the ribs to show the crowd that he was real.

"Ouch!" exclaimed Luan.

She didn't pay the slightest bit of attention to his reaction. All that she cared about right now was the massive pile of diamonds she was about to receive on selling him!

"Let's start the bidding at three thousand diamonds. Do I hear three thousand?" she said, cupping her ear to the crowd.

There was no stopping the women now, especially when Luan had forgotten all about his beauty spot, which just happened to be on full view for the *entire dwairy world* to see.

The dwairy women were going crazy, smacking on lipstick and bidding all of their diamonds in the hope that they would get the chance to kiss him.

Luan watched them in horror.

He rattled the bars of the cage, hoping he could break loose and escape, but the bars wouldn't budge. He didn't know what to do. He stuck his hands into his pyjama pockets, clenching his fists bravely. He was getting ready to take a swipe at whoever was first to open up his cage. He felt something cold and smooth against the sweating skin of his palm. He pulled it out to have a look.

"I recognize this!" he said, flipping the delicate piece of golden jewellery from hand to hand.

"It's, it's ..." He opened up the locket and took a peek inside. A glittering cloud of magic dust blew up in his face, making him remember. "It's mum's locket of remembrance that I took from her for good luck!"

All the past flooded back to him at once, and he remembered every single tiny detail of his life.

He looked up at the excited crowd again, his hand automatically being raised towards his beauty spot.

"Uh-oh", he groaned uneasily, putting Anna's locket of remembrance round his neck this time for safekeeping. "Everybody can see my beauty spot!" Luan wiped the beads of sweat dripping from his forehead. He suddenly realized the terrible danger he was in.

An
Encounter
with
a
Clairy

6

"Going once, going twice and sold to the woman in the black cloak for thirty thousand diamonds!" the black-heeled dwairy yelled, jumping up and down in excitement. She had never sold anything for so much money in her entire life. She was going to be oh so very rich!

The entire crowd of women sighed aloud all at once, bitterly disappointed that their dreams of taking Luan home with them were utterly ruined. They turned around, heading for home, sniffling sadly all the way.

"I wish it was as easy for me to turn around and go home", he thought to himself.

Only one woman remained. 'The woman in the black cloak', as the black-heeled dwairy had called her. The woman to whom Luan was bound to the chains of eternal slavery. He squinted, trying to get a good look at her through the glare of the sun as she waddled towards him. She was pushing a wheelbarrow of sparkling diamonds in front of her and seemed to be dragging something fluffy and pink behind her.

The black-heeled dwairy's eyes lit up when she saw the diamonds. She plunged her hands into the middle of the wheelbarrow and let them slip through her fingers gleefully.

"I'm rich, I'm rich, I'm so very rich", she sang at the top of her voice, dancing round in circles.

"Aren't you going to let me out of this cage?" Luan asked her before she got completely carried away with her new-found wealth. But as soon as she did let him out, and he found himself face to face with his new mistress, he decided that he would have been much happier staying in the monkey cage for the rest of his life!

Luan's new mistress was so hideous to the human eye that he hardly dared to look at her. He would glimpse at her for a split second and then look away in disgust.

It was the very same hideous hag that had bought the sulky woolly pig earlier on, he was sure of it. And the pig had an even sulkier expression on its pink face now, if that was possible, as it trotted wearily along behind her. Luan knew *exactly* how it must feel - just the same as he was feeling right now!

The black-heeled dwairy didn't seem too happy to be near the cloaked woman either, and at the first opportunity she got, she raced off in the opposite direction with her wheelbarrow of diamonds.

He tried to gulp back his fear, and be polite to his new mistress; after all, she might be a very nice person on the inside. His mother had always told him how important good manners were.

"I'm Luan Shee and I am *very* pleased to meet you", he lied as he put out his hand to shake hers.

But she didn't shake it.

She didn't seem to have any manners at all. She just started frothing at the mouth like some sort of wild animal.

"I hope she doesn't try to bite me", Luan said to himself. "Things are bad enough without me getting big chunks of my body bitten off!"

The woolly pig looked scornfully up at him and rolled its eyes. Luan could have sworn that it had understood what he was thinking.

He decided to introduce himself again; maybe she hadn't heard him the first time. "I'm Luan Shee and I am *very* pleased to meet you", he lied once more.

She must have heard him this time because she opened up her mouth into a sort of a half-smile, half-frown, showing off a mouthful of yellow teeth all filed into points like the serrated edge of a saw. Her lips were all scabby and bloody from the sharp teeth digging into them.

Luan and the woolly pig looked at each other in horror.

She wore thick brown woolly tights in the blistering sunshine. Both Luan and the woolly pig had to hold their noses with the stench, Luan with his fingers and the pig with his trotter.

The hag threw Luan onto the pig's back without warning, and hopped on behind him herself, gathering her cloak up around her. She gave the pig an almighty kick in the bum with her big black boots to make it go faster, and it squealed and squealed all the way.

She was hugging Luan so tight that he thought she might squeeze him to death.

Luan was fed up with her not talking or answering his questions. He would just have to use his own brain to find out as much as he could about her.

"She's not a dwairy, because she isn't tiny or wearing high heels to make her look not-so-tiny", he decided.

The pig was nodding its head.

"Hmm, and she's definitely not a fairy because she looks nothing like my mother".

The pig cleared its throat.

"Ahem, ahem!"

It sounded like it wanted to say something, but it didn't get a chance because as soon as it opened its mouth, it got another kick in the bum!

"I must be going mad!" thought Luan. "Everybody knows that animals can't talk!"

All of a sudden strange noises started to gush out of the woman's mouth.

"Ooh ooh aah aah!" she said, sounding just like a monkey woman! Luan understood her even less than he understood Seersha's baby talk, and *that* was saying something.

She kept on making the same 'Ooh ooh aah aah!' sounds non-stop, and Luan couldn't get so much as a word in, to let her know that he had no idea what on earth she was talking about!

Then she became even more like a monkey, beating her chest excitedly with her fists and dribbling all over his nice pyjamas.

He sat still as a statue, hating every second of his journey on pigback, but he daren't try to push her away for fear of what she might do to him.

She didn't look like the type to mess with.

The woolly pig began to pant heavily under their weight. It didn't seem to be the fittest animal in the world. "But then I don't suppose pigs were designed to do the work of a horse", Luan thought, "or were they? On second thoughts, I don't suppose there's anything that says they can't!" he decided.

The pig squealed again.

The three travellers plodded across many fields, up many hills and down many slopes until they finally arrived in the depths of a forest, where not a creature stirred. They entered a lonely dark maze of shadowy trees, where every single tree looked exactly the same. It was bad enough luck being bound to the chains of eternal slavery with this gruesome hag, but the fact that Luan didn't have the slightest clue where he was or how he was going to escape from such a place made matters seem so much worse.

"But I have to escape no matter what. I have to rescue Seersha from nasty Grandma's fairy fort before it's too late", and there was no changing his mind.

In the very heart of the forest stood a lonely shack, with shadows dancing all around it.

The very sight of it sent a shiver down his spine.

There were life-size stone statues dotted all along the forest path leading up to the shack. The statues looked exactly like humans and Luan could have sworn that they *really were* humans once upon a time, because the painful expressions chizzled into their faces looked so *very* real.

Luan was starting to feel more uncomfortable than ever. An appalling idea began to take shape in his thoughts - suppose, just suppose he would end up being turned into a stone statue for all eternity too! It didn't bear thinking about.

Suddenly, the hag tumbled off the exhausted pig, breaking into hysterics of 'Ooh ooh aah aah!', picking Luan up and swinging him round and round in the air in some sort of welcoming ceremony.

Then she started to waltz with her unwilling and frightened partner, until she was so dizzy that they both toppled onto the ground with a thud.

The woolly pig held his trotter over his little mouth and was sniggering away to himself behind it. It made a change from his sulky expression, that's for sure!

Up jumped the hag again, none the worse for her fall, picking Luan up and hurling him head first into her shack. She booted the squealing pig in on top of him.

The door was quickly bolted behind them and the familiar 'Ooh ooh aah aah!' could be heard growing fainter and fainter in the distance.

"Phew!" said Luan, relieved to be rid of her, even if it was only for a short time. He badly needed some time to himself to plan his rescue mission.

"If I hadn't met that weird Dwaireen Dwairy woman, I would have come up with a great plan ages ago", he said to himself, shaking his head.

"Well at least I've made it to Teernoman in one piece, that's always a good start", he thought, doing his best to look on the bright side of things.

He began to get used to his new home, although he hoped he wouldn't be staying there for too long.

The hag in the black cloak's little shack was just like her. It was damp and gloomy, mouldy and smelly. A row of woolly tights were hanging on a washing line from one side of the room to the other, with all sorts of rotting fungus and poisonous mushrooms growing out of them. He wondered if that was why she had bought the woolly pig at the auction of eternal slavery - to make more tights with his wool, that is. He didn't think she would find any other use for a slow sulky woolly pig.

"I beg your pardon!" a very cross voice answered his thoughts. Luan looked all around him anxiously.

There was no one there.

Except, of course, the pig dusting his trotters after the fall, and a jar of maggots in the corner of the room.

"Have some manners, my boy, and look at me when I'm talking to you", came the cross voice once again.

Still no sign of anyone.

"Right, that's it! If you're not willing to look me in the eye when I'm talking to you, my boy, well then I'm just going to have to make you!"

Luan felt something nipping his fingers.

"Ooouuuch!"

"Well it serves you right for being so rude. Didn't your mother ever teach you any manners?"

Luan stuck his fingers into his mouth to ease the pain. He looked down to see who had bitten him.

And there was the woolly pig, looking up at him with his big eyes, sulky as ever.

"You didn't have to bite me", said Luan becoming just as sulky looking himself.

"Well I did try to get your attention, my boy", the pig answered. "Maybe we got off on the wrong trotter. How about we start again, my boy?" Luan thought that was a good idea, even though he felt weird talking to a woolly pig of all things!

"Sheepig's the name, my boy, Sheepig of the Sty. I'm not a sheep and I'm not a pig, I'm a sheepig if ever there was one, and a rare breed we are in these parts! And I don't take too kindly to being called 'the woolly pig' either, I'll have you know. That's highly insulting".

"But I didn't call you 'the woolly pig', well, not out loud anyway", Luan replied looking puzzled.

"Ah yes, but you did call me that in your mind, didn't you? Yes you did and don't try to deny it!"

"How could you know that?" Luan asked, getting more and more puzzled by the second.

"I, my boy, have a rather useful magical gift. I'm an expert mind-reader. I studied it at university I'll have you know. Fascinating subject!" Sheepig boasted proudly.

Luan didn't know whether to believe him or not. He certainly didn't look like he was joking.

"Right", said Luan, deciding to put Sheepig's mind-reading gift to the test, "if you can read minds like you say you can then tell me what I'm doing here".

"Hah!" thought Luan, "that'll fix him. He'll never be able to answer that one!"

Sheepig shook his head. "It's a sad thing when youngsters like yourself don't believe what their elders tell them", he sighed. "Now where shall I begin? Hmm". He started to sing.

"You've left your mother and cozy home,
To search for Seersha all alone,
You've crossed the fierce and ferocious sea,
Ending up in a shack with me.

You've found yourself in a clairy's den,
Staring out at statues of men,
You're keen to fight Queen Danu the Great,
But may end up as mince on her plate!

"How was that, my boy, are you satisfied now that I'm telling the truth?" he said, beaming up at Luan.

Luan was in shock.

"Wow! I'd better be careful what I think in future, you never know who could be listening to my mind", he announced after a long silence. "Quite right, quite right you are, my boy", Sheepig agreed.

"So, if you can read my mind, does that mean you can read the mind of our mistress?" Luan asked doubtfully.

"Of course I can", Sheepig replied, snorting arrogantly at such a silly question.

"Would you mind telling me about her then, what she's thinking about and all that stuff?" asked Luan, suddenly fascinated by Sheepig's strange magical gift.

"Certainly, my boy, but only after you tell me what your gift is. Fair is fair. I told you mine first, so now I want to know yours". Luan didn't quite understand.

"But I don't have any gifts like that!" he exclaimed, shocked that the thought had even crossed Sheepig's mind.

"Of course you do, my boy, everyone has a magical gift".

"Well, everyone says I'm the best player on my football team at home, does that count as a magical gift?" Luan asked doubtfully.

"Certainly not, my boy! We're not talking about *ordinary* gifts here; everybody in the world has *ordinary* gifts. No, no, no, we're talking about *magical* gifts. If your mother is who you say she is, and if your Grandma is really Queen Danu the Great, then you most certainly have inherited a magical gift. We'll just have to visit the Gift Doctor to find out what your gift is, if we make it out of here alive".

This was far too much for Luan to take in all at once.

It seemed strange to him that his mother would forget to tell him something as important as what his magical gift was.

"Maybe she didn't forget to tell you, my boy, maybe she was waiting to tell you when you were older, so that you would use it more wisely, for a magical gift can be a terrible burden to bear if it isn't used wisely", Sheepig said philosophically.

"Now, back to more pressing matters, my boy. I don't suppose you have the faintest idea what a 'Clairy' is for starters, being a human and all that?"

Luan shook his head.

"Oh", he said, an idea entering his head all of a sudden, "has it anything to do with a dwairy or a fairy, the names all sound alike anyway?!"

"Well, my boy, you are on the right track, I suppose", said Sheepig, settling down on a wobbly chair to tell his story. It creaked beneath his weight, and then collapsed completely! A cloud of dust blew up around him, but nothing was going to stop him telling his story.

"A clairy is in actual fact a cloned fairy gone terribly wrong, and that's exactly what our new mistress is, I hate to say".

He shuddered at the very thought of her, while blowing the dust out of his way.

"Hold on, Sheepig, I know what a fairy is, but what's a clone?" asked Luan, all ears.

"Do they teach you *anything* in those human universities of yours?" asked Sheepig in disgust at Luan's lack of knowledge.

"But I'm far too young to go to university yet!" exclaimed Luan, pleasantly surprised that Sheepig had thought he was old enough and clever enough to go to university. But Sheepig wasn't listening. He preferred to hear the sound of his own voice.

"A clone is an exact copy of something else. Every single little bit of it, right down to the tiniest detail, is exactly the same as the thing it was copied from. Understand now, my boy?"

Luan nodded.

Sheepig continued his explanation.

"I don't really know how clairies came to be, to be perfectly honest with you, my boy, but I do know that they are hatched out of big blue eggs on clairy farms in the wilderness. My cousin Pigshee used to work in one of them. The clairy farms are surrounded by huge iron walls to keep the clairies locked inside, because they can be very dangerous beasts indeed when they are fully grown, but a few always manage to escape, I'm afraid".

"Did our clairy mistress escape then?" Luan asked, filled with horror.

"I suppose so, my boy, I suppose so".

"There are many different rumours about how they came to be", Sheepig continued, enjoying Luan's reaction to his story, "but I will only tell you the most believable of all the rumours". Luan was taking in every single word Sheepig uttered.

"A tenth cousin of a friend of a friend of a friend of my cousin Pigshee told him and he told me".

"Hold on", said Luan, "that's way too hard to understand! Can you say it more simply please?"

"Very well", said the storyteller, becoming rather impatient. He wasn't half as good at telling stories as Luan's mother was.

"Queen Danu the Great only had one daughter, that being your mother Anna Shee, and she ran off with your human father, as you know, not that I blame her, mind you! Queen Danu was outraged. She plotted a horrible revenge to punish your mother for her disobedience. She began to make armies of clones of herself with the help of the best scientists in Teernoman. She planned to send the clairies to the human world to kill your mother. But they went horribly *wrong*, my boy, and when I say *wrong*, I mean *wrong*", he said, looking gravely at the boy.

"She trained them in combat, with guns and swords and bombs in the clairy farms, but they were wild beyond belief, even wilder than the wildest wolves. They turned not just against her, but against everyone else as well. They were a danger to the very scientists that created them. So they were locked into the farms, and no fairy will enter a farm again until they are quite sure that every last clairy is dead". Luan was speechless.

"I can't believe nasty Grandma is *that* nasty", Luan said after a long silence.

"*Nasty* Grandma? Who is *nasty* Grandma, my boy, and what has she got to do with my story?" Sheepig asked, all puzzled.

"Nasty Grandma is Queen Danu the Great, of course!" Luan exclaimed, expecting Sheepig to know such basic things.

"Oh! Well! I suppose that makes sense, my boy!"

"And nasty Grandma stole my little sister and I'm going to her fairy fort to rescue her and bring her home to mum, but you know all that already because of your magical gift, don't you?!"

He made it all sound so simple.

"Hmm, I knew bits and pieces from reading your mind, my boy, but now it all makes perfect sense! We'd better find a way out of here, if a determined young fellow like you has such a great mission ahead of him!"

"How about we try to dig our way out?" suggested Luan.

"Typical human idea!" Sheepig snorted. "Didn't your mother ever teach you any magic at all, *even* the basics?" Luan thought hard, eventually shaking his head.

"Well, *you're* in luck, my boy. I just happen to be an expert magician, studied it at university I'll have you know!"

Luan wondered if there was anything Sheepig *hadn't* studied at university. It sounded like a fascinating place!

Of course, Sheepig failed to mention one very important fact about studying magic at university - the fact that he had failed every single magic exam he had ever sat!

"Now, what sort of a spell should we cast, my boy? Use your brain if you humans have one".

"How about, how about we put a spell on the clairy's shack to make it fly to nasty Grandma's fairy fort? You could do that, couldn't you, Sheepig?" Luan asked hopefully.

"Certainly", Sheepig replied. "Easy peasy!" He seemed quite sure that he knew what he was doing.

"Right, first things first, my boy. Now, do you see that slab of rotting meat over there? Yes, that one", he said, pointing to the higgledy-piggledy shelf. "Drop it into the clairy's cauldron. Very good! Now add that and that and that and a handful of maggots, not too many, my boy, careful! Careful does it! And now add that and that ..."

Sheepig was busy ordering Luan all over the dark room, instructing him to throw all kinds of horrible things into the clairy's cauldron. He certainly didn't want to dirty his own trotters in the process! "What is the clairy going to do with us if we don't have the magic potion ready by the time she gets back?" Luan asked, trying to catch a mouse scurrying under a filthy rotting floorboard.

Sheepig suddenly became silent.

"Sheepig? Sheepig?"

"We're already bound to the chains of eternal slavery, so she can do what she likes with us", he sighed.

"But what will she do with me, Sheepig?"

"She'll keep you as her husband".

"*Husband? Husband?*"

Luan didn't believe his ears. "But I'm only a boy, I can't possibly be her *husband!*"

"Try telling her that! You can blame it on that beauty spot of yours! Then, when you're a grown-up, she'll turn you to stone so that you'll never grow old. That way she'll have you to love forever and ever".

"Like the statues on the path?" Luan asked, so terrified that the hairs on his arms and head stood straight up into the air. Mind you, he didn't know which he was more terrified of - being her husband or being turned to stone.

"Wha-wha-what will she do with you?" he stuttered.

Sheepig didn't answer.

"Shee-Sheepig? Sheepig?"

Sheepig started to sob.

"She's going to - she's going to boil me alive", he sniffed. "Sheepig stew for dinner! Sheepig tongue for desert! Sheepig ears for supper! Sheepig trotters for midnight snack!"

Sheepig became more and more hysterical the more he thought about his future.

"She's gone to find vegetables to cook in the pot with me now", he wailed.

Luan pulled down a pair of tights from the washing line, giving it to Sheepig so that he could wipe his eyes and blow his nose. "Come on, Sheepig, cheer up. If we use your great magic then there's no way she'll be cooking Sheepig stew or Sheepig tongue. And besides", said Luan, "I bet Sheepig tongue is *revooooolting* to taste!"

Sheepig snapped back to his usual ways on hearing such an insult. "I'll have you know that Sheepig tongue has a *sumptuous* taste, my boy, *it's* a delicacy, *and* Queen Danu's favourite food, so don't you dare insult it!!"

"What else do we need for your spell?" Luan asked, trying to get Sheepig to focus his attention on something slightly more important!

"That'll do", he huffed, "now be quiet while I concentrate". He began to chant a spell in the magical ancient Gaelic language, waving his front trotters soothingly over the clairy's cauldron:

"Imi! Imi! i wad i gayn
Imi a tigeen go rah Danu,
Imi le Sheepig is Luan Shee,
Imi le splanc tintree!"

("Go, go, head far from here,
Go to Danu's fairy fort, little shack,
Go with Sheepig and Luan Shee inside you,
Go with a flash of lightning!")

73

Sheepig's chanting sounded very good to Luan, but then he didn't understand a single word of it! And it was indeed very good chanting, because he only made one little mistake. But that little mistake just happened to change the spell entirely!

Instead of saying 'Imi le shee gweetha', which means 'Go with a gust of wind', he had said to 'Go with a flash of lightning', and all of a sudden a huge flame leaped out of the cauldron, jumping so high that it set the roof ablaze. Sheepig didn't jump out of the way in time and very nearly scorched his trotters.

"Why I *still* can't get my spells right I just don't know", he muttered under his breath, shaking his head in disbelief.

"Em, I don't mean to bother you, Sheepig", said Luan, quite calmly in the circumstances, tapping Sheepig on the shoulder as he gazed at the roof. It was quickly becoming engulfed in flames.

"In case you haven't noticed, we are standing in a room that is on fire and if we don't get out very quickly, the clairy will be eating *barbecued Sheepig tongue*!!!" he roared in his ear.

That brought Sheepig straight back to his senses like nothing else could.

"It wasn't my fault!" he squealed, trembling in fright at the mention of barbecued Sheepig tongue.

"The spell - the spell is to blame – it - it played a trick on me!"

Luan didn't have time to listen to his excuses.

The clairy would see the smoke billowing up through the sky and would be back in minutes. He didn't think she would take too kindly to having her home burnt down or her entire supply of woolly tights cremated! Why, she might even be eating barbecued Luan tongue if he wasn't careful.

There was only one thing to do.

"Give me a hand here, Sheepig!" Luan coughed through the smoke. He lifted up the clairy's cauldron with all his strength and flung it out the one and only dirty little window in the shack. The window smashed into little pieces. He thought he might just about fit through it, but he wasn't so sure about Sheepig!

Sheepig was no help at all. He might be a grown up Sheepig and Luan might only be a human boy, but right now, Luan was by far the more mature of the pair.

Sheepig was dancing round the shack, swaying all over the place in his efforts to prevent his precious woolly coat from catching fire. Luan grabbed him by the ear, and hauled him over to the window, squealing all the way. This was going to be the tough bit.

He tried to lift him.

He tried to push him.

He tried to shove him.

He even tried to kick him.

But it was no good, he just wouldn't budge.

All of a sudden, the front door of the shack was flung wide open. Low and behold Sheepig jumped into mid-air, sailing effortlessly up and out through the little window, making sure to save his own skin! *There* stood the clairy, breaking into a frenzy of madness, as she threw her burning treasures out of her way in her attempt to grab hold of her escaping prisoners.

Luan made a dive for the window, and he was *so* close to making it through. He was just dragging his feet through it when he felt a firm hand gripping him and tugging him from behind. The clairy had lunged halfway across the room, managing to grab his ankles.

"Help me, Sheepig!" he roared, frightened out of his wits.

Sheepig pulled himself together and grabbed Luan's arms and began to tug him from the outside. The clairy began to tug him from the inside and, within seconds, a tug-of-war was in full swing between the two of them. One huffing and puffing and going 'oink!oink!', the other coughing and spluttering and going 'ooh, ooh, aah, aah!' in their efforts to claim poor Luan for themselves.

Luan felt like they had been tugging him for hours and hours and he was quite sure that if his hands or feet didn't come flying off at any second, he would certainly be a good ten inches taller by the time they had finished stretching him! While Luan was thinking about his body being stretched like an elastic band ready to snap, the fire was still blazing away in the shack, getting bigger and hotter all the time.

The cloaked clairy had no way of protecting herself from all the sooty smoke billowing around her and she soon became wheezy and dizzy. She loosened her iron grip ever so slightly and Sheepig could feel it.

This was his big chance. He took a massive breath, until his cheeks were so full of air that they looked like two big pink balloons.

Sheepig tugged like he had never tugged before.

Luan's body came toppling straight down on top of him like a ton of bricks. They both groaned aloud in pain and exhaustion. A shrill shriek grated on their ears from behind. They turned their heads just enough to see the roof of the shack caving in and the walls collapsing below it.

Massive flames gushed from the cloaked figure of the clairy as she fell in a heap to the ground. They watched on in silence, their eyes glued to the horrendous scene. They knew so well that the heap of embers glowing through the darkness could just as easily have been their remains.

Fantasy
Falls

7

Luan awoke at the break of day, but he didn't know that it was daytime because the forest was so very dark.

He thought about his mum and little Seersha. He wished he could send Anna a starletter, just to let her know that he was well and that he missed her very much. But he couldn't even see the sky through the trees, never mind finding a star. And even if he could see the sky *and* find a star up there, well, he still didn't know how to go about taming it!

Sheepig woke up beside him with such a powerful snort that his snout began to run.

"I beg your pardon, my boy, but you wouldn't have a handkerchief by any chance, would you?" he asked Luan.

Luan shook his head.

"Suppose I'd better go find one then, my boy", he said absently. He was still half asleep.

"Yeah, I'd better get going too", said Luan, picking himself up off the forest floor. "I've got to rescue my little sister, but it was very nice to meet you, Sheepig", he called as he walked off. He hadn't gone far when he heard the pitter-patter of feet scurrying up behind him.

"This maze of trees is no place for a youngster to be wandering around alone, my boy", Sheepig announced, catching up with him. "And besides, you're going to need a clever university graduate to help you on your mission", he added.

The truth of the matter was that Sheepig would be frightened out of his wits if he had to wander around the forest all alone, but he was far too proud to admit it.

The remains of the clairy's shack were just out of view, when Luan thought of something very important.

"You know those human statues outside the clairy's shack, Sheepig?" Sheepig nodded.

"Well, is there any way, any way at all of bringing the men trapped inside the stone back to life?"

Sheepig looked deep in thought.

"No", he finally said.

"Are you sure?"

"No, I never studied *that* at university. I suppose that if we smashed the statues, then the spirits trapped inside could be freed, my boy, but I couldn't be sure".

"Let's try it then!" called Luan with enthusiasm, already turning on his heel and running back.

He raced up the path, with Sheepig power-trotting behind him. The statues were still intact.

"You take the statues on this side of the path, Sheepig, and I'll take the other", Luan instructed.

"We'll have a race! Ready? On your marks, get set ..."

Sheepig had begun already.

"Go!"

And off Luan went, pushing and shoving and doing his best to smash every single statue into tiny pieces, trying to catch up with the cheat! But it wasn't the impact of the stone statues hitting the ground that cracked and shattered the statues, despite what Luan and Sheepig believed. It was in fact the simple touch of their warm-blooded fingers, which held the power to break the Clairy's cold-blooded spell.

A look of sheer delight lit up both of their faces as they watched a spirit rise out of each and every broken statue. The smiling spirits all joined hands and floated high into the sky, free for all eternity. Luan and Sheepig forgot all about their race, they were so busy gazing at the results of the good deed they had done.

"Job well done, my boy, job well done", Sheepig said, patting Luan on the back.

It was time to press on once again. They had no more time to waste if they wanted to make it to Queen Danu the Great's crystal fort before it was too late.

After trotting round in circles for hours, after much whining, huffing and complaining (all on Sheepig's part), the pair of voyagers stumbled out of the maze of trees quite by accident.

Sheepig stepped out into the sunshine, only too glad to feel its warm glow on his face after being stuck in the stuffy forest for so long. He could see nothing but grassy green fields for miles and miles around. There wasn't a clairy or a fairy or ever a dwairy in sight.

Luan was right behind Sheepig.

They could still see the happy spirits plunging and diving through the wispy clouds high above them, enjoying every second of their newfound freedom.

"You know, Sheepig, my nasty Grandma can't be *that* nasty if she can create a world as beautiful as this", Luan remarked at this point, gazing at the many wonders of nature surrounding him.

"Ha!" snorted Sheepig in reply, "don't be deceived by the appearance of beauty, my boy, for its sole purpose is to hide a bitter ugliness deep within the foundations of our land. The apparent beauty and freedom of Teernoman is no longer true beauty nor true freedom, a sad fact that you shall realize with the passage of time and the gaining of wisdom, my boy". Sheepig's big words and attempts to sound cleverer than he was went totally over Luan's head, but he didn't suppose it had too much relevance to his rescue mission anyway!

All of a sudden Sheepig stopped in his tracks, refusing to budge. Luan was getting used to his ways, realizing that sometimes he could be the most impulsive and stubborn Sheepig ever!

"There's something that has to be done before we go a step further or else it's going to land us in all sorts of trouble", he announced, sounding all serious and furrowing his brow.

Luan wondered what was wrong with him this time.

"What's wrong with me this time, my boy? You should remember that *I* can read your mind!" Sheepig said rolling his eyes as if he was talking about the most obvious thing in the world.

"What's wrong with me, you ask? I'll tell you what's wrong with me! *Your beauty spot of course!*" he roared into Luan's ear.

Luan knew he was right. His beauty spot had had a terrible effect on all the dwairies at the market, not to mention his narrow escape from his clairy mistress.

"Well, how can I get rid of it then, Sheepig? You should know".

Luan was waiting for him to boast that he had studied the art of removing beauty spots as well as everything else in university, but, to his surprise, he didn't even mention it.

"I'll have to burn it off, it's the only way", said Sheepig, examining the beauty spot closely, "unless, hmm, unless I try a little bit of magic ..."

"Noooooooo!" Luan butted in. Who knows what would happen to him, if Sheepig's last magic spell were anything to go by! "Why don't we just stick to burning it off. It's not *too* painful, is it?" he asked doubtfully.

"Leave it to doctor Sheepig, my boy, and all will be well!"

That was exactly what Luan was afraid of.

"Oooouuucch!"

"There we go, bingo!" Sheepig said trying to pat himself on the back with his trotter but it just didn't reach far enough.

Luan bit his lip, trying hard not to cry. He didn't know if he was in shock or in pain. But then he felt a stinging sensation, and he knew for sure that it was pain he was feeling. His skin felt like it had been cruelly peeled open like an orange, layer after layer.

The tears welled up in his eyes, but he was determined to be brave and not to let them escape.

Sheepig, meanwhile, had given up his attempt to pat himself on the back and was busy prancing around Luan in circles, brandishing what looked like a smouldering magic wand to Luan's watery eyes. "Hey, that's not fair, you tricked me, Sheepig, you said you wouldn't use any magic on me", Luan said in disappointment.

"I beg your pardon!" Sheepig snorted, turning from pink to purple with anger.

"This!" he said pointing to the magic wand, "is simply a branch of burning wood, Mr Luan (he used the term 'Mr Luan', instead of 'my boy' whenever he was cross). The surgical instrument used for your *highly successful* operation might I add!"

"Sorry, Sheepig", said Luan meekly. The last thing he wanted to do was anger Sheepig when he only wanted to help him.

"That's alright, my boy, you're forgiven", he said, calming down and turning back to his usual shade of pink again, "but do be quiet, my boy, you never know who could be spying on us in these parts".

Luan looked around him suddenly feeling very uneasy. Off set the pair of voyagers once again, venturing into the unknown. Luan hopped on Sheepig's back just as he began to sing again:

"Beautiful you will no longer be,
From the love of women you are set free,
And the sheepig you have to thank is me,
Now you are free, my boy, Luan Shee!"

Luan had to laugh at Sheepig. He felt an enormous weight had been taken off his shoulders now that his beauty spot was gone.

"Oh no!" Sheepig exclaimed out of the blue.

"What's wrong?" said Luan in alarm, thinking it was something serious.

"I should have *cut* off your beauty spot, my boy, instead of *burning* it off. That way I could have stuck it onto my own face and watched all the lovely lady Sheepigs back in the sty fighting over me", he said, shaking his head at his stupidity.

Luan burst into fits of laughter, until his sides hurt more than his burnt skin. He couldn't help it. The very idea of Sheepig with a big black beauty spot stuck to his face with a lump of sticky tape or glue was so ridiculous that it was enough to make anyone laugh!

They plodded cheerfully over the vast carpet of newly cut soft green grass that was still stretching for miles and miles in front of them. Luan hoped they were headed in the right direction to reach nasty Grandma's crystal fairy fort.

He took long deep breaths. He loved the fresh smell of the countryside.

The sun was still beating down, quite a different scene from his drizzle-drooped homeland.

"It's so nice to be able to see the sun shining", he announced. Sheepig threw him a strange glance.

"What's so nice about *that?*"

"At home it's always damp and raining".

"Do you mean to say that in the human world it *isn't* summer all year round?" Sheepig asked in shock.

"Do *you* mean to say that in Teernoman it *is* summer all year round?!" Luan replied, equally shocked.

"Obviously, my boy, unless Queen Danu fancies taking Teernoman on one of her sailing trips across the many oceans of the world. Nobody ever knows what sort of weather to expect under those circumstances! Mind you, I'm glad to say that doesn't happen too often anymore".

"Look here, my boy, the flowers are always in full bloom, the birds hatch out of their eggs every day of the year and the fruits on the trees are always ripe". Sheepig was pointing his trotter at the one and only tree in sight, a huge towering tree with glossy green leaves, so big that they were the size of umbrellas.

He scurried up the tree without the slightest bit of bother. (His secret of course was that a thorn staircase was sticking out of the trunk, because Sheepig would never be able to climb a tree like that just using his little trotters!)

"What fruit would you like from the Sweet-Tooth Tree?" he called down from his perch high up in the branches.

"The Sweet-Tooth Tree!" thought Luan, peering up and up but seeing no sign of Sheepig. "What a delicious sounding name! What sort of fruit grows on it?" Luan called back, suddenly realizing how hungry he was.

The Sweet-Tooth Tree began to quiver and shake with the help of Sheepig.

Luan felt something thump him hard on the head.

A shower of fruit rained down on top of him as he tried to duck for cover. He looked around him, surprised as ever.

There were clusters of chocolate-coated apples and toffee-coated pineapples and honey-coated cherries and sugar-coated berries of every kind heaped up high around him.

"Wow, a tree that has every type of fruit on it, now that's what I call a cool tree!"

Sheepig landed back on the grass with a thud, licking some sticky toffee off his trotters.

"It is rather a 'cool' tree as you say, my boy. Only pity is that there are very few Sweet-Tooth Trees left in the world".

"Why's that, Sheepig?"

"Greediness I'm afraid", said Sheepig sadly.

"Queen Danu is felling the trees so that she can use their bubble gum to make weapons of mass destruction".

"Bubble Gum? I don't see any bubble gum", Luan remarked, looking at the tree above him.

Sheepig proceeded to take a big bite out of the tree trunk. He chewed the bark a bit then blew a massive bubble that burst, covering his entire face with sticky gum.

Luan was shocked. He had never imagined, not even in his wildest dreams, that there was such a thing as an edible tree.

"Fancy a picnic, my boy? Come on, follow me and we'll dig in!" Luan didn't have to be asked twice.

Sheepig climbed the thorn staircase with Luan right behind him this time, licking the trunk and the leaves and the sticky branches as he went. Sheepig's stomach had been growling like a grizzly bear ever since he had smelt the sweet fruit on the breeze. "Back in the sty I used to eat a six course meal six times a day", he boasted, licking his lips. The sty sounded like such a wonderful place that Luan wondered why on earth Sheepig had ever left it in the first place. He definitely didn't want to talk about that though, so he switched the topic of conversation the first chance he got.

They seemed to be climbing up forever, until at last they came to a huge empty marshmallow nest at the very top, where Sheepig proceeded to make himself comfortable on a bed of candyfloss feathers. A loud cracking sound came from underneath him. He rolled over on his side, pulling a broken chocolate egg out from under him.

"A woolly, talking pig that lays eggs!" Luan exclaimed, pretending to be shocked, even though he knew there was no way Sheepig had laid that egg. Or maybe he had. After all, Luan knew perfectly well at this stage that what his mother always said was true, that everything *was* possible in Teernoman!

Luan sprawled out gleefully, biting into a massive strawberry. Its sweet juice gushed out as he munched happily away, and much to his delight there was a big lump of solid strawberry ice cream in the middle of it, just waiting to be licked! It was exactly what he needed to cool himself down on a hot summer's day. He had never tasted anything so good.

"Is there any way I could grow a fruit tree like this at home, Sheepig?" he asked, licking away to his heart's content.

"Well, my boy, I don't suppose there's any harm in taking a few pips from the Sweet-Tooth Tree home with you. If you sow them and water them and feed them every day, you might just have a Sweet-Tooth Tree in your own garden before very long. You should take pips from the fruit at the top of the tree, as it gets the most sunlight and is the juiciest fruit of all!" Sheepig replied. "I just hope your teeth won't rot!"

Luan was at the treetop already, struggling to pull a caramel-coated apple off a branch. It was firmly stuck to the branch and didn't seem to want to budge at all, but Luan wasn't going to give up on getting his pips for his own Sweet-Tooth Tree without a fight.

"Yes!" he said in glee, as it finally broke off, the effort of it all very nearly sending him toppling down to the hard ground beneath. He munched and crunched away at the apple until he got to the core. Then he popped the smooth brown pips into the locket of remembrance for safety, and dreamed of his garden back in BallyBoo, covered in Sweet-Tooth Trees!

"Take a look at the view while you're up there!" Sheepig called from the shade of the bird's nest, chuckling away to himself while he lay back, twiddling his pedicured trotters.

Luan looked all around him. What he saw was so extraordinary that he forgot all about the pips at once.

North, south, east and west he looked.

He could see *everything*.

Absolutely *everything* in the *entire* land of Teernoman.

He could almost touch the spirits they had freed, which seemed to be hovering above them wherever they went now.

He could see the fluffy cotton clouds puffing by in the sky, the waves crashing against the rugged coast, the tiny dark forest where the clairy had imprisoned them far behind him, the iron walls of clairy farms in the distance, the little villages speckled over the vast sprawling green fields in front of him, and most importantly of all, he could see Queen Danu's Crystal Tower of Light, in the very middle of her fairy fort, in the very middle of a circle of smoking volcanoes. The sheer brightness of the tower almost blinded him.

Sheepig had crept silently up behind him, wearing a pair of sunglasses that he had pulled out from under his woolly coat. He looked like a movie star! He beamed at Luan's shocked, squinting face.

"You knew about this view, didn't you, Sheepig?"

"General knowledge, my boy, general knowledge, some of which you will have to acquire before you come face to face with Queen Danu the Great, that's for sure! But have no fear, my boy, the Gift Doctor will have revealed your magical gift by then, and *that*, at least, might help you to rescue your sister".

"Do you think I'll be able to see the *entire* planet Earth from the top of the Sweet-Tooth Tree that I'm going to grow in my garden?" he asked Sheepig, in awe at the very idea.

"I don't see why not, my boy, I don't see why not!"

Luan was delighted. Things had started to go so well for him ever since they had left the clairy's forest behind them. He pulled the map of Teernoman that his mother had drawn the night of his departure out of his pyjama pocket. It was all yellow and crumpled and dog-eared after his adventures, but he could still just about make sense of it.

He traced his journey on the map with his finger, looking up from time to time to make sure he was on the right track.

"Of course, you do realize, my boy, that the Crystal Tower of Light is hundreds and hundreds of fairymiles away".

Luan's face dropped.

"But it's just over there, right beside us!" he said pointing his finger in its direction but not daring to look at it for fear of being blinded.

"The strength of its light deceives you, my boy", said his friend, shaking his head slowly.

"Well", replied Luan, slightly disappointed that he wouldn't be able to complete his mission and return home just yet, "at least we know in which direction we have to go. That's a good start. Come on, there's no time to lose!"

And off he went, jumping down the thorn staircase with Sheepig hot on his heels.

The friends pressed on, full-tummied and hot and sweaty. Sheepig, feeling generous, even agreed to give Luan another piggy-back, or a 'Sheepig-back' as he insisted on calling it.

Luan didn't seem to know the terrible danger that lay ahead of him, especially being a human boy, and that was worrying Sheepig. All was well while they were still alone in the wilderness, but as soon as they bumped into some fairies (which could be very soon as the Feast of the Full Moon must be over by now), he knew perfectly well that there would be trouble lurking for the young and brave Luan Shee.

He decided he would have to teach the boy some magical tricks of survival before long, unless they were lucky enough to bump into the Gift Doctor on their travels, although that was rather unlikely. The Gift Doctor wasn't known to stray any further than one side of her surgery to the other, and that was far away in Queen Danu the Great's fairy fort, where the Queen could keep a close eye on her.

After many long hours of trotting along and watching the graceful spirits circling overhead, the companions began to wonder why the spirits hadn't embraced their freedom and flown to faraway skies.

"They must have some unfinished business to attend to, my boy", was the best answer Sheepig could come up with, and Luan agreed with him as he couldn't think of a better answer himself.

Then Luan spotted a river flowing in the distance. It was the river that his mum had drawn on her map, and he had seen it from the top of the Sweet-Tooth Tree.

"Fantastic!" he exclaimed, slapping Sheepig to make him go faster. Sheepig didn't take too kindly to being slapped or bossed around by a human boy of all things, and he slowed down on purpose, just to teach Luan a lesson. But Luan didn't notice in his excitement, and he hopped off Sheepig's back, racing across the fresh grass until he reached the riverbank.

Sheepig, not wanting to be left alone as usual, caught up with Luan, huffing and puffing and heaving all the way. His woolly coat went from a candy-floss shade of pink to a deep cerise colour with all the sweating. He sat down at the edge of the bubbling water to bathe his blistered trotters.

He began to mumble something about 'Fantasy Falls' when Luan spotted his massive pink bum sticking up into the air.

Maybe if Luan had bothered to listen to Sheepig's mumbling, he could have avoided a lot of trouble, but as it happened, he just couldn't resist the urge that sprung to his mind.

With a mischievous glint in his eye, Luan crept up behind Sheepig, giving him an almighty kick in the bum that catapulted the poor sheepig into the middle of the river with an enormous splash.

Luan put on an innocent face and began to look around him as if someone else had kicked Sheepig.

"Are you alright, Sheepig?!" he laughed. But Sheepig wasn't alright.

What Sheepig had been mumbling about was 'Fantasy Falls', the greatest waterfall in all of Teernoman, and it was just a little way downstream. It was a deceptively beautiful place, with danger lurking beneath its veneer of purity. Anyone who was daring enough or foolish enough to fall down the waterfall would see their greatest fantasy in the water at the bottom of it. But, if they did not pull themselves away from their fantasy, they would drown in it, and never see the light of day again.

Sheepigs weren't made for swimming, but that thought had never even crossed Luan's mind. Of course, if they *were* born to swim, they would have been given gills and slinky scales and fishy tails instead of a snout and wool and a useless excuse for a tail that was good for nothing, except maybe decorating with a ribbon for special occasions.

Sheepig was in big trouble. His sunglasses had gone flying downstream for starters. His little trotters were splish-splashing at a ferocious rate against the gushing current as he struggled to catch hold of the glasses. His woolly coat began to weigh him down like a lump of lead, and his little snout was bobbing up and down, down below the surface where it filled up with so much water that he couldn't breathe.

The river grew swifter and swifter as it approached Fantasy Falls and Sheepig was halfway downstream with only his two little ears sticking up out of the water by the time Luan realized what was happening.

"Oh no, what have I done?" Luan groaned, overcome with horror. "Why didn't I think first?"

He ran along the riverbank as fast as his newly stretched legs could carry him, ripping off his pyjama top as he went. He dived deep into the water, plunging swiftly forward as if he had lived his whole life in the water.

His eyes scanned all around him, looking for a glimpse of pink that would lead him to Sheepig.

No luck.

He was too busy to notice the pressure of the gushing water building up as he got closer and closer to Fantasy Falls.

Onward he swam, suddenly spotting exactly what he was looking for. Luan grabbed at Sheepig's stumpy tail with a firm hand, pulling it back towards him with all his strength, until he had a good grip on Sheepig's whole body.

He lifted his companion's head out of the water, ready to give him the kiss of life, although he really didn't like the idea of kissing a sheepig! Luan struggled to lift his own head above water.

At last he managed, just in time to see Fantasy Falls looming large in front of him.

He gulped back in terror.

There was no escape.

He squeezed his eyes shut as tightly as they would go, while Sheepig clung on to him for dear life, his nails embedded deeply in Luan's youthful skin.

Down they toppled, down and down.

The water gushed on all sides, frothing and spitting in all directions, and sucking them into the treacherous waters of Fantasy Falls.

And then, all of a sudden, they reached the bottom of the waterfall and everything was calm again. The water started to bubble cheerfully in the sunshine as if nothing out of the ordinary had happened.

Sheepig and Luan were in the heart of the danger zone, and Fantasy Falls was working its powerful magic on their little minds ...

Sheepig was back home in the Sty. He was sitting on the royal throne and his subjects were showering him with roses and gifts, bowing to him and kissing his trotter in respect. He wore a solid gold coat that shone so much that it was as bright as the sun. And there was the beautiful Queen Sheepig by his side, radiant as ever ... there wasn't a happier animal or a better King in the whole wide world.

Meanwhile, Luan was back in BallyBoo, doing exactly what he loved best.

There he was in the middle of the sandy football pitch, dribbling the ball towards the goal. He was moving faster than lightning and, no matter who tried to tackle him, he still had possession of the ball. There was no stopping him now! He could see a little girl and a man and a woman cheering him on from the sideline. They all looked so familiar.

It was Seersha, with long hair like her mum's, and there was dad and mum right beside her.

"Go on, Luan, score!" they yelled and yelled.

Luan kept running towards the goal. The goalkeeper was snarling and spitting at him as he approached. It was nasty Grandma! Nasty Grandma was the goalkeeper!

He looked down at the ball getting ready to strike it as hard as he could. But wait a minute - he wasn't kicking a ball at all. He was kicking none other than a beating heart with '**Queen Danu the Great**' printed on it in big bold letters. He had found nasty Grandma's heart. *He* and *only* he had the power to turn her into a nice Grandma! And there was only one way of putting her heart inside her where it belonged. He would have to score a different sort of goal with it - a goal that would pierce her skin, and land in the middle of her chest! He took a deep breath and lobbed the heart right at her, with all of his human skill.

His head went muzzy.

He couldn't see if he had scored his goal or not.

He wished he could know for sure.

He tried to run towards nasty Grandma to see, but something was pulling him back.

His mum and dad called his name "Well done, Luan! You've given nasty Grandma a heart at last!" They looked so happy. He *had* to stay with them to celebrate, but he was being pulled away so hard ...

Not a soul was stirring at the bottom of the waterfall.

The spirits had been hovering high in the sky, waiting for the right moment to attend to their unfinished business. The magic of Fantasy Falls was too powerful and too beautiful and too tempting for its victims to ever want to leave it.

But the spirits had joined hands in mid-air, as Luan and Sheepig had watched them do before, and plunged into the water to wrestle with the force of magic, and just in the nick of time.

Sheepig and Luan struggled and kicked and punched and wailed in their desperate attempt to remain part of their most wonderful fantasies, while the spirits did their best to drag them back into the land of the living.

All sorts of splashing and thrashing was going on between the spirits and the travellers far beneath the clear surface of the water.

All of a sudden three ghostly spirit heads popped up out of the still water, followed by two pink ears. Then a little snout, sneezing, spluttering and coughing all the way. They floated to the riverbank, carrying Sheepig between them, and left the exhausted animal on the soft grass to recover.

Seconds later up popped three more spirits carrying a weary Luan to the riverbank. He was still calling out to his family. "Don't let them take me, mum, I don't want to leave!" he wept inconsolably.

The spirits gathered together and soared high into the sky again, their final task completed.

Slowly but surely Luan came back to his senses, although he was a little dazed for a while. "That was the weirdest dream I've ever had!" he said, trying to remember all the details. "Don't think I'll be going swimming in that river again, mind you!" he said, turning over to face Sheepig.

Sheepig's breathing was quickly returning to normal and all was well, considering how close he had come to death. Luan suddenly remembered that *he* was the cause of their frightening experience and whispered a very guilty 'sorry' in Sheepig's ear, and how he meant it. Sheepig was none the worse for his bath in the river but he insisted on making a fuss about it.

"If you had listened to a word I said instead of playing silly tricks, Mr Luan, none of this would have happened. It's just as well that I studied the art of swimming at university and was able to save your life".

"But you didn't save my life or even your own life", thought Luan, pointing up to the smiling spirits in the sky. "It was them".

"Well, well, well", uttered Sheepig wistfully as he watched the spirits disappear into the horizon. "I must have been right about them having some unfinished business to attend to, but I didn't think it was anything to do with us".

Luan and Sheepig lay basking in the glorious sunshine, watching the skies open up to welcome the spirits.

They waved goodbye, both relieved and fully aware that they had the spirits to thank for saving them from the terrible magical powers of Fantasy Falls.

Buttercup
Surprise!

8

All this time, while Luan was on his great adventure, there were no such adventures going on back in BallyBoo. Had Anna Shee been an ordinary mother, she would have been so sick with worry that she would have been driven to madness with the grief of losing her husband and her children. But luckily for Anna Shee, she was no ordinary woman. She wasn't going to give up on her children's safe return without a fight, even if their return was against all odds. And so she continued to send starletter after starletter to Cara Shee, trying to find out what had become of her children. Seersha, she was aware, was in the hands of Queen Danu the Great, but even more worryingly, Cara had no news of Luan. She did inform Anna that his boat had been found drifting in the middle of the Atlantic Ocean, but that was all she knew.

He could easily be at the bottom of the sea.

Chances were that he would never find Seersha and make it home safely. It just wasn't possible for a human boy to hide in Teernoman, especially one with a cursed beauty spot.

Queen Danu the Great would have him torn to shreds and fed to Olkas her pet monster, but at least Cara had promised to look after him if she did find him, which gave Anna the tiniest ray of hope. She simply *had* to believe her son was still alive despite everything, and, with that positive frame of mind, Anna sent him a useful starparcel under the care of Cara Shee.

Not one of the neighbours in BallyBoo came anywhere near her cottage to see if she was so much as alive. They avoided her more than ever, as if she had some deadly contagious disease that they would catch if they even looked at her.

Anna had thought about telling the police that her son was missing. But what would they think if she told them he was missing in the fairyland of Teernoman? They would probably decide she was mad and lock her up, and if her children ever *did* return home safely, then they would be taken away from her and put into care. And that would never do. No, it was best not to tell them.

Meanwhile, Sheepig and Luan were blissfully unaware of Anna Shee's sleepless nights far away in BallyBoo.

They had gathered themselves together and were back to their usual form after their narrow escape from the magic of Fantasy Falls. Luan was busy making sure that his Sweet-Tooth Tree pips were still safely hidden inside his mother's locket of remembrance, while Sheepig was busy complaining again.

"Just look at my poor woolly coat, my boy", he said with disgust. "It has turned into a great big ball of fluff!" It really did look like a big ball of fuzzy fluff now, Luan thought, but he didn't think Sheepig would be too happy if he agreed with him!

This side of the river was very different from the other one. Luan felt like he was looking at everything through a magnifying glass. He hoped Fantasy Falls hadn't made them shrink. Maybe everything just grew to a bigger size on this side of the river because the soil was better. That's what he had learned in school anyway, he thought, shrugging to himself.

As far as the eye could see, they were surrounded by fields of giant multi-coloured flowers swaying gently in the early evening sunshine. Their smell reminded Luan of his mum's perfume.

"It looks like we're just on the edge of Buttercup Glen", Luan announced to his companion, studying his map which was still soggy, thanks to Fantasy Falls. The ink on it had got smudged too, which made it terribly difficult to follow.

But, thanks to the spirits, they were still on the right track.

The companions had a good long look around them, taking in the scenery. "Got a starcard from here once", Sheepig mused. "Very famous place".

"How could you get a starcard when there's not a person in sight to send one!" Luan exclaimed, assuming a starcard was much the same as a human postcard.

"Who says a starcard has to be sent by a person?" Sheepig snapped quickly, pointing to the busy-looking insects flying round. He was right and Luan knew it.

The butterflies fluttering by were the size of kites and even the odd toadstool they came across, half-hidden between the thousands of flowers, was big enough to sit on. Luan jumped on top of an orange toadstool, which let out a huge puff of laughing gas in his face. He couldn't stop giggling for ages, much to Sheepig's great annoyance!

The companions darted forward, zigzagging under the shade of one flower to the next, half scared that some giant bird with a hungry belly would spy them and swoop down to eat them. Sheepig secretly hoped that they would catch Luan instead of him, convincing himself that the boy looked far juicer and far tastier to the eye than a bony Sheepig like himself!

"Sheepig?" Luan asked inquisitively.

"No!" Sheepig replied.

"But how can you say no before you hear my question?" Luan asked in annoyance.

"You forget that I can read your mind, my boy. I know perfectly well that you were going to ask me if I have ever met your nasty Grandma. Well, am I right?"

Luan nodded.

"Like I said, my boy, the answer is NO! No, thank goodness", he added.

"Is she really as nasty as I've heard she is? Will she brainwash Seersha so that she doesn't remember me or mum or dad?" Luan inquired.

"Nasty she is, my boy, and I dare say, although I dread to think it, she is already in the process of brainwashing your little sister, so we'd better get a move on before we're too late to save her".

That was the last thing that Luan had wanted to hear, but he knew it was the truth.

"I'm not quite certain how we're going to get into Queen Danu's fairy fort either", Sheepig mused aloud. "They say she's got evil spies everywhere in the land, waiting to capture the likes of us! Still, we'll deal with that problem when we come to it, my boy", he said, patting Luan fondly on the back. Luan shuddered at the thought of 'evil spies'. He knew only too well what terrible things they had done to his father on *his* first trip to Teernoman.

Without warning, there were no more flowers to hide them.

They stopped, overlooking a cliff with a sheer drop of a thousand fairyfeet. They cast their bulging eyes down and down, gasping at the sea of gold stretching for miles below them.

It was Buttercup Glen, without a shadow of a doubt.

"Woohoo!" Luan shouted, his echo rebounding across the length and breadth of the Glen. "We're still on the right track!"

Kissing Anna's pendant of remembrance for good luck, he dived head first over the cliff, tumbling and stumbling and somersaulting through the air until he landed right bang in the centre of the Glen, sending giant petals flying in all directions as he thudded to the ground.

Sheepig, being less adventurous, and not wanting to break his nails, found himself a winding snowdrop-speckled path leading into the Glen. He trotted along with the grace and posture of a royal sheepig. Luan was awaiting his arrival.

"Welcome my friend, *Atchoo! Atchoo!*" Luan sneezed, popping up out of a flowerbed with swollen red eyes and a runny nose.

"Goodness gracious, my boy, what has happened to you?" asked Sheepig, studying Luan's symptoms with intense interest.

"*Atchoo!* Hay *Atchoo!* Hayfever*", Luan just about managed to reply.

"But there's no hay here!" Sheepig snorted comically.

"There doesn't need to be", Luan replied, "it's the pollen in the *Atchoo!* buttercups that causes it".

"Why isn't it called *pollen*fever then?" asked Sheepig, all confused. Luan came up with a good argument.

"Well, *hay*fever is like buttercups, they're called *butter*cups but they aren't *really* cups of butter. They're just words that don't actually mean what you might think they mean!"

Luan was very impressed with his explanation of hayfever. He'd have to remember it to explain to Seersha when she was older.

Sheepig, however, was more confused than ever.

"I'm afraid I don't have the slightest notion what you're trying to tell me, my boy. Buttercups are most certainly cups of butter, so *hay*fever must be caused by hay".

"How could they be cups of butter when everyone knows they're just flowers? *Atchoo!*" Luan laughed.

"Do you want to make a bet?" asked Sheepig, looking deadly serious.

"Yes, only I don't have anything to bet with", said Luan.

"If I win, promise me you'll help me return to the Sty, my boy".

"And if I win, Sheepig, promise me you'll help me save my little sister".

"Deal?"

"Deal!"

They shook hands on it.

"Now, my boy, look and learn!"

With that, Sheepig reached for the nearest flower, tilting the top of its stem towards him and taking a long refreshing slug of melted butter from it.

Luan followed his example despite his shock.

The butter was rich and sweet and dreamy and creamy, nothing like the cow butter he smeared all over his toast at home.

"Who would ever have thought it! Cups of butter from buttercups", he gargled between gulps and sneezes. "This land is getting stranger and stranger the more I get to know it!"

They did their best to catch every last drop on their tongues, licking their lips to capture the droplets that had managed to escape. Luan was busy savouring this delightful treat with his eyes shut when Sheepig let out a dreadful high-pitched wail.

Luan's eyes flapped open, immediately recognizing the danger note in Sheepig's voice.

Sheepig was still near Luan, they were only separated by a few flowers. That was a relief. But he seemed to have something round his neck and his face was turning blue.

Luan pushed the flowers aside to get a better look. He could see a rope round Sheepig. And it was being pulled tighter and tighter round his chubby neck.

"Who is it, who's there?!" Sheepig shrieked frantically, attempting to turn his head around to see. But try as he did, he couldn't budge it.

Luan's eyes followed the direction of the rope, until they arrived at the other end of it. There stood a rough humanish-looking girl. Her face and hair were covered in butter, and her body was scrawny and green like the stalks and leaves of the buttercups. Standing behind her was an entire gang of identical girls with their arms folded. They didn't look the friendly sort.

"That can't be right", Luan said to himself. "There aren't any humans in Teernoman except me, but come to think of it, those can't be human girls because their heads are stuck on back-to-front!" he suddenly realized.

Little did Luan know that Sheepig was up to his usual tricks and was reading his companion's mind for clues as to the identity of his captor. The back-to-front girl with the rope, who was clearly the leader of the gang, started to talk to Luan. She sounded very angry, but Luan couldn't understand her anymore than he had understood the Clairy, which wasn't very much at all!

Much to Luan's surprise, Sheepig seemed to have understood every word the girl had said and was trying to answer her in her own language. He was sounding equally angry.

The two began to snap and snarl at each other, so Luan decided to jump in between them before they started a fight. A fight would be the last thing they needed right now, especially when they wanted to draw as little attention to themselves as possible.

"What on earth's going on, Sheepig?" Luan asked, fed up being kept in the dark. Sheepig took a quick break from his snarling to answer him.

"Should have known something like this would be just our luck, my boy", he groaned. "What you see before you", he said, snarling between words, "is a butterbabe, bound to the chains of eternal slavery to protect the buttercup's butter. And she isn't too happy that we've been helping ourselves to a little refreshment after our tiresome journey".

Luan stayed silent for a moment, finally saying, "But if she's bound by the chains of eternal slavery just like we were, should she not be on our side?"

"You would think so, my boy, but butterbabes aren't on any side except their own sly, selfish, twisted one. They care about nobody or nothing except themselves. On second thoughts, that's not true. They're said to be friends of Queen Danu the Great, but she's as horrible and selfish as they are. Mind you, my boy, if your head or my head was twisted like a butterbabe's, we would probably have twisted minds like theirs too!"

Luan didn't like the sound of these butterbabes standing before his eyes.

"What's she saying to you and why can't she speak our language?" Luan wanted to know.

"She does speak our language, her sentences are just back-to-front like her head. Listen, my boy".

Sheepig was right - understanding the butterbabe just took a little bit of concentration and practice.

"sdnomaid derdnuh eno em yap uoy sselnu gipeehs eht eerf t'now I", said the butterbabe, pulling the rope as tight as it would go.

Sheepig began to choke.

Luan thought hard for a minute, before being able to make sense of the sentence front-to-back.

"I've got it!" he said triumphantly. "'I won't free the sheepig unless you pay me one hundred diamonds', that's what she said!"

"Uh-oh", he added, as the meaning sunk in.

"Huh, I'm worth far more than a measly one hundred diamonds", said Sheepig, disgusted at such a cheap ransom being demanded for him.

"But we don't have any diamonds", Luan replied apologetically, ignoring Sheepig's silly comment. He was getting the hang of talking back-to-front.

"We're very sorry for tasting your butter, we thought it was wild and that anyone was allowed to drink it".

Suddenly they all had to duck for cover from a huge bumblebee buzzing as loud as a helicopter, which was flying in their path. It only just missed them.

"Huh!" grumbled the butterbabe leader, springing back to her upright position. "Is it not perfectly clear to you stupid creatures that these buttercups are perfumed and polished by an expert every single day?! Finest butter in the whole of Teernoman it is.

Even Queen Danu the Great orders it by the fairygallon". The rest of the butterbabe gang behind her nodded their heads in agreement.

The butterbabe leader hauled the squealing Sheepig towards her, studying him with interest.

"You know, the nights can get a bit chilly here sometimes. Queen Danu sends a bitter breeze from the east to punish her fairy enemies by freezing them to death".

Luan shivered at the very thought.

"So I could do with a nice warm woolly coat. What do you say, sheepig? Hand over your coat or you and your weird-looking friend will be my prisoners forever more. It's your choice".

Sheepig's body stiffened. There was nothing in the world that he cared for more than his woolly coat. He looked at it sadly, then at Luan, then at the coat, and from one to the other again and again and again. It seemed like an easy choice to Luan - one woolly coat was a small price to pay in return for freedom, but Sheepig was a lot more attached to his coat.

"Take it!" he finally sobbed, big tears rolling down his face. He tried his best to be brave when the butterbabe pulled a shears out of the tool bag on her back and began to chop and slash away at his lovely pink fluff. She snipped a bit here and snipped a bit there, so skillfully that the job was done in seconds.

Sheepig darted off into a thicket of buttercups as soon as he was set free, mortified by having to stand stark naked in front of Queen Danu the Great's grandson of all people! The butterbabe laughed cruelly at the embarrassed animal, before picking up her nice new coat and doing cartwheel after cartwheel, until finally disappearing from view, just as quickly as she had appeared in the first place. Her gang disappeared behind her in the same manner, well camouflaged by their colouring.

Luan waited for Sheepig. He could hear him sobbing and fumbling about nearby, but he couldn't actually see him.

"Come on, Sheepig, I've got to go, and so do you if you want me to help you find your way home to the Sty!"

No reply.

"There's nothing to be embarrassed about. Sure, where I come from pigs have no woolly coats at all. They're always naked and nobody minds!"

Still no reply.

"You don't look as ridiculous as I do in my pyjama bottoms!" he called, looking down at himself.

Luan couldn't wait any longer.

Precious time was ticking by, and the butterbabe leader or her gang might even have alerted nasty Grandma to their whereabouts. "Sheepig, I'm leaving you right now", he called, stamping his foot to let Sheepig know that he meant business. "I hope you make it back to the Sty without meeting any more clairies!"

That should do the trick!

And it did.

Just as he had expected, Sheepig scurried towards him through the undergrowth. But he looked completely different now.

He wasn't naked anymore.

He had made himself a coat of green leaves all patched together. He looked as ridiculous as ridiculous can be. But there was no way Luan could tell him that, or they'd never make it out of Buttercup Glen.

"Nice coat, Sheepig", he lied. "The green in it really suits you". Sheepig beamed from ear to ear on receiving the compliment. "Yes, my boy, I do believe the green shade brings out the lovely colour of my eyes".

Luan had to disguise his laughter as another fit of sneezing.

The sky was beginning to darken, casting wispy shadows over the sea of gold and marking the onset of twilight. Luan wanted to keep going. There would be plenty of time for rest after his rescue mission had been completed. Twilight always reminded him of his mum back at home.

Suddenly, an idea struck him.

"Sheepig, you know how to send starletters, don't you?"

"Of course, my boy, any citizen of Teernoman who cannot write a starletter should hang their head in shame. It's the very first thing we learn", he replied.

"Could you teach me how to send one to my mother then, if it's not too much trouble?" Luan asked hopefully.

"Certainly, my boy, certainly. We'll have to wait though, until the lazy stars begin to shine. Honestly, sometimes they're so lazy that they don't even bother to ... good grief, would you look at that!" he exclaimed, changing the conversation.

He was pointing at a big butter bubble rising high into the sky, and popping aloud. It burst, disappearing into nothing.

Luan spotted the next butter bubble doing exactly the same thing 'pop!'

Then they both spotted the third bubble and the fourth and the fifth and then a whole cluster of bubbles of all shapes and sizes rising all at once. They seemed to be rising out of a buttercup. Even Sheepig had never heard of a bubbling buttercup before!

"A little peek won't do us any harm, what do you say, my boy?" They had already got themselves into enough trouble to last them a lifetime, but one thing that the citizens of Teernoman and humans have in common is that they're extremely curious by nature, and neither Sheepig nor Luan Shee were exceptions to this rule.

"Just a little peek then", Luan agreed as he tiptoed silently towards the bubbling buttercup. He began to peel back the petals of the half-closed flower, before it snapped closed, almost cutting his nose off. Naturally enough Sheepig had let Luan take a peep first, just in case there was any danger involved.

Jumping back in shock, Luan let out an astonished gasp. He landed on Sheepig's trotter behind him. Sheepig put his sore trotter into his mouth to ease the pain as he tried to balance on three legs. He wasn't too successful and toppled over on his side, banging his head.

He seemed a bit dazed. For a split second he thought he heard the bubble-blowing flower giggle.

"I must have got a terrible knock on my head, my boy. Ha! I could have sworn that I heard that buttercup giggle just there!" he said, shaking his head sadly at his own madness to think such a thing.

"You did!" laughed Luan. "There's a little fairy girl blowing bubbles inside the buttercup, look!"

Sure enough, up popped a little fairy head out of the cup, complete with hat, scarf, gloves and coat. The little girl was smothered in butter and she was giggling at the funny sight of Sheepig in his leaf coat. She had a mischievous little face with sparkling eyes.

"She looks just like my little sister", Luan said, picking up the sticky little lady, "but my sister doesn't wear a hat and scarf and gloves and coat in the sunshine! I wonder why she's wrapped in so many clothes?!"

"What's your name, young lady?" Sheepig asked her in a serious grown-up voice.

She began to giggle all the more.

"I don't think she understands you, Sheepig. Before nasty Grandma stole my little sister she couldn't understand me either. She was too little", Luan replied simply.

"Well she *has* to have a name, my boy, it's rude not to address her by her name".

"Why don't we call her Bubbles then?" Luan suggested.

"Bubbles, Bubbles, Bubbles", said Sheepig, gazing at the little face. "Yes, I think it suits her", he decided.

"Well Bubbles, it has been a pleasure meeting you but we happen to be on a very dangerous rescue mission right now, so I'm afraid we'll have to say goodbye", Sheepig announced, shaking her sticky little hand, although he would rather not have done so.

He began to trot onward.

Luan caught up with him, still holding Bubbles.

"But, Sheepig, we can't *possibly* leave Bubbles where we found her. She must be lost, and what if the butterbabes or a giant bumble bee found her?" he said, aghast at the very idea of leaving the little lady all alone as night was falling fast.

"We'll have to take her home".

Sheepig didn't look too happy.

"What about our rescue mission, my boy? You don't have time for silly games like this!" he huffed.

"This isn't a silly game", Luan replied calmly. "If my little sister was lost, I would want someone to find her and bring her home, so that's exactly what I'm going to do. I'll just have to wait a while to complete my rescue mission, that's all".

Sheepig began to sulk, but there was no changing Luan's mind. He was determined to bring Bubbles home to her mother, even if that meant he wouldn't reach nasty Grandma's fairy fort before she got a chance to brainwash little Seersha.

Some things in life just had to be done, and this was one of those things.

Luan noticed a clever little gadget strapped to Bubbles' wrist. It looked a bit like a watch, but it had a big letter 'H' in the middle of it and an arrow pointing out from it.

On second thoughts, it looked like a cross between a watch and a navigator's compass.

He wondered what it was for. It was quite a confusing little gadget really.

"That, my boy, is a home-detector", Sheepig informed him, realizing that his sulking was getting him nowhere.

"A home detector?" Luan repeated, looking at it all puzzled.

"All the fairy children in Teernoman have them in case they get lost like Bubbles here. See, 'H' stands for 'Home' and all they have to do is follow the direction of the arrow and it will guide them straight home".

"What a brilliant idea!" Luan exclaimed. "If I could make a home-detector when *I* return home, then I could be a millionaire as well as saving the Sweet-Tooth Trees from extinction in my garden, and me and mum and Seersha could live happily ever after!" he squealed in delight, already dreaming of the great future that would lie ahead of him upon his return to BallyBoo.

Ice
Town

9

There were no cars or buses or trains in Teernoman. Not because they hadn't been invented there but because when there was eternal life there, nobody ever needed to rush, except Luan and Sheepig, of course.

Time was ticking quickly by in Luan's homeland, while he was busy doing his best to complete his rescue mission. As a result of this, Luan and Bubbles had no choice but to travel by 'Sheepiggy-back' which was ever so slightly faster than walking. They grabbed onto his ears to steady themselves.

They plodded through the blackness of the night, without the light of the moon or the lazy stars to guide them.

"Those stars must have taken a night off after the Feast of the Full Moon", Luan heard Sheepig mutter crossly at one stage.

Bubbles had been all excited when she met the funny looking strangers, and she was even more excited when she got to ride on Sheepig's back.

She was able to say one thing, and one thing only, they discovered, and that was 'giddy-up, horsie!'

She said it over and over again, slapping Sheepig's back with her sticky buttered hands.

"I beg your pardon, young lady, but I am certainly not a 'horsie' or anything like it. I am a pedigree Sheepig. Tell her, my boy", Sheepig snorted, disgusted by such an insult.

"She doesn't understand you!" Luan laughed helplessly.

Bubbles giggled her cheeky little giggle all the more whenever Sheepig spoke, making him more and more furious. But she soon got bored, as little girls do, and she started to hum a lullaby in her sweet baby voice.

Before long Luan and Sheepig had joined in and she nodded off to sleep. It made the journey seem shorter.

Luan kept a close eye on Bubbles' home-detector, but it wasn't too easy to see in the dark. Still, as long as they followed the arrow, everything would work out just fine.

They had left Buttercup Glen far behind them and were surrounded by a very different landscape, although they were barely aware of it at first. They felt the temperature drop very suddenly and huddled together for warmth. Then they spotted snowy-topped mountains looming large in the distance. The whiteness of the mountains shone through the blackness.

Sheepig soon found himself crunching over a carpet of ice with the weight of his load. They shivered all over, the only noise to be heard being their teeth chattering in the freezing cold. They wouldn't be able to survive here for long ...

The 'H' on Bubbles' home-detector suddenly lit up, shining through the darkness. She was back in her homeland.

"Thank goodness!" Sheepig croaked, watching the steaming warm air from his mouth rising up through the cold night air around him. "Now to find her mother and quickly, my boy", he added. It was times like this that his leaf coat was no good to him and he dearly missed his woolly coat, although he shouldn't have been complaining when Luan had no coat at all to keep out the bitter cold.

Luan nodded, too cold to open his mouth.

The three travellers continued to follow the arrow of the home-detector. Bubbles was blissfully unaware of the cold, all wrapped up and sleeping peacefully in Luan's arms. They followed the arrow along a narrow winding path, until they could see a row of twinkling lights ahead of them. They had arrived in a fairy town.

Sheepig didn't want to go any further. He had never been in this fairy town before and he didn't think the fairies there would be overly welcoming towards them.

"Come on, my boy, we've obviously taken a wrong turn, let's go back", he pleaded with Luan, but Luan wasn't having any of his nonsense.

"This is Bubbles' home. Look, the home-detector says so! We've *got* to go into the fairy town".

They were shocked by what they saw shining through the darkness. There they were, standing in the middle of a winding fairy street, where everything was made from ice.

The twinkling lights they had seen from the distance were really rows of twinkling ice-bulbs hanging from the rooftops brightening up the streets. Even the shops and houses and trees were carved out of big blocks of ice. They couldn't believe their eyes.

"I thought you said it was always summer in Teernoman", Luan whispered, half-afraid of what he was seeing.

"It *is* always summer in Teernoman", replied Sheepig, looking more than half-afraid.

Somebody must have heard their whispering because all of a sudden a window was flung open and a cheeky fairy face appeared, all wrapped up in a hat and scarf. Somebody else must have heard that window opening because another one opened straight away, then another and another, until there were faces peeping out of every window and door and keyhole in the town. Multi-coloured icicle lights were switched on, making it so bright that it felt like the middle of the day.

Luan saw a snowball coming towards him, and he ducked, letting it wallop Sheepig's head. Bubbles woke up with all the commotion and began to cry.

Suddenly hundreds of Eskimo fairies appeared on the street out of nowhere.

They had heard the voice of the mayor of Ice Town's lost daughter and came out to welcome their little fairy girl home. They were dressed in hats and gloves and big woolly scarves that Sheepig admired with envy.

A fairy with long long silver hair skated forward to greet them. She was the mayor of the village.

"Mamma", called Bubbles in glee, stretching out her arms.

"Thank you so much for finding my baby", said the fairy woman, hugging her little daughter. "My people and I will repay you for your kindness in whatever way we can".

With that, she took Bubbles from Luan and led the tired travellers through the town, her hair trailing like a veil behind her. Luan and Sheepig had to do their best not to step on it.

Fairies had lined the streets, and were cheering and clapping and whistling as they passed them by. Sheepig's head swelled up so much with all the attention he was getting that Luan was afraid it would burst.

Luan tried to catch up with the mayor.

"Your village is very beautiful but icy cold", he said to her. He reckoned that mentioning the weather was always a good way to start a conversation.

"My magical gift is to warm people's hearts, and as long as their hearts are warm, the cold outside doesn't bother them", she said, smiling at the human boy.

"And what is your magical gift, young man?"

"I don't quite know yet", he replied honestly. "Sheepig says I have to go to the Gift Doctor to find out!"

The mayor nodded her head in approval. "The Gift Doctor is a very learned woman, if a little crazy! She will teach you how to use your gift well", she said, deep in thought.

Luan noticed that her skin was as pale as the snowflakes silently trickling down on top of them and her eyes were as blue as the bottom of Fantasy Falls.

"But my friend Sheepig told me that it's *always* summer in Teernoman unless the island is sailing past the North Pole or some other cold place. So how can one part of Teernoman be warm and another part be cold at the same time, it just doesn't make sense?" he continued, wanting to return to their previous topic of conversation.

The mayor sighed deeply.

"It used to be summer here in Ice Town once upon a time, when I was a little girl", she said quietly.

"What happened then, my dear?" Sheepig piped up, suddenly interested in their conversation. They hadn't even realized he had been listening.

"Then, then Danu became queen and everything changed. She was cruel and ruthless and horribly selfish".

"Go on", said Sheepig, impatient for her to get to the point of her story. The mayor took her time despite Sheepig's impatience.

"One day Danu was on a picnic in Ice Town, or Sun Town as this place used to be called a long time ago. She was only a spoilt young girl at the time and she wanted an ice-cream.

There wasn't any.

She *demanded* an ice-cream.

She screamed and yelled, but it made no difference.

'When there aren't any ice-creams there isn't a lot you can do except make one', she shrugged.

So that's what we did. Every fairy in Sun Town helped to make the biggest and creamiest ice-cream ever tasted, just to keep the new queen happy. But by the time we had finished making it for her, it had melted in the sun.

She got so mad that she turned the entire town into ice. She said that that way there would be plenty of ice-cream for her to eat the next time she decided to come here for a picnic".

Luan couldn't believe his ears.

"She didn't?!" he said in horror.

"Oh yes she did", replied the mayor.

"Queen Danu turned your town to ice *just* because she couldn't get an ice-cream that didn't melt?" he said in disbelief. He couldn't get his head round such a nasty thing to do.

"Still, that's a long time ago, best forgotten I suppose. How about a midnight feast, would you like a midnight feast to help my people celebrate the safe return of Bubbles?" the mayor inquired of her guests.

She didn't have to ask twice.

The mayor of Ice Town flung open two ice doors, leading into a massive banqueting hall. The ice table in front of them was heaped with every kind of cold food imaginable.

There were mountains of ice-cream of every flavour, froghurts (frozen yoghurts), chocolate friscuits (frozen biscuits) and frakes (frozen cakes). The friscuits and frakes didn't sound very nice, but as soon as the travellers popped them into their mouths, the heat melted them into the most deliciously sweet and crunchy vanilla chocolate flavour they had ever tasted. It was even tastier than the fruit from the sweet-tooth tree, and that was saying something!

Luan and Sheepig were placed on ice thrones at the head of the table alongside the mayor, where they were waited on hand and foot. Waitresses skated by them on their ice skates, carrying trays of milkshakes in ice glasses.

"Let the festivities begin!" announced the mayor, clapping her hands three times from her throne, and everyone began to stuff their faces with the delightful food.

A fairy dressmaker, whose magical gift was the ability to knit anything imaginable in the blink of an eye, skated towards

Sheepig and Luan. She took out her tape-measure to check their sizes. Then she pulled out two knitting needles and a ball of wool from inside her coat, and knitted hats and gloves and scarves for them, just like the ones she was wearing.

Sheepig was watching her thoughtfully.

Her hands moved as fast as lightning.

"You couldn't knit me a woolly coat while you're at it, could you, my dear? It is frightfully cold after all", he couldn't stop himself from asking.

No sooner had it been said than it was done.

He fitted on his new woolly coat for size, along with his matching hat, scarf and trotter gloves.

"It's a little tight but it will do, my dear", he announced after inspecting it closely. He grinned from ear to ear.

Bubbles was sitting up in her ice high-chair beside her mother, dribbling chocolate ice-cream all down her face as she tried to blow bubbles with it. Her mother stood up as soon as people began to grumble that their bellies hurt from eating too much.

"A little bit of exercise is the only way to feel better", she announced to the two travellers with the bulging bellies by her side.

She stood up, clapping her hands three times once more.

A troop of musicians and dancers appeared.

Before long everyone had joined in, and Sheepig, getting carried away, even sang a song in his operatic voice, while everyone else clapped along:

"La la la la la, la la la la la,
Nothing in this world compares to the Sty,
Not even lady Sheepig, the apple of my eye,
Nothing in this world could take me away,
Not even a Sweet-Tooth Tree on a hot summer's day.
La la la la la, la la la la la,
Nothing in this world compares to the Sty,

121

Not even Mother Sheepig, with her tasty apple pie,
Nothing in this world will make me content,
Not unless I reach the Sty before my life is spent.
La la la la la, la la la la la,
La la la la la, la la la la la!"

Everyone clapped and cheered as Sheepig bowed in all directions. He secretly thought that Ice Town *did* compare to the Sty, and that in actual fact, it was *even better* than the Sty, but he couldn't possibly admit that after singing his song.

Sheepig and Luan stayed up until dawn, watching iceworks crackling high above them and lighting up the night sky.

Much later that morning, (although it didn't seem like much later because the sun never shone in the sky in Ice Town), Luan Shee woke up. He was all snug and cozy in his new woolly clothes. But he couldn't remember where he was at first.

He rubbed his eyes, looking around him. He seemed to be swinging. He *was* swinging, swinging in a hammock made from soft snowflakes all knitted together. There were rows and rows of empty hammocks around him, hanging from ice encrusted trees. He reckoned he must have been in an ice forest.

He rolled over on his side, not expecting to be greeted by a pink snout snoring in his face. He felt something smooth rubbing against his skin. The locket of ...

"Oh no", he groaned, still only half-awake. He jumped up and shook Sheepig beside him.

"Come on, Sheepig, we've got to leave right now to finish our rescue mission, or we'll be too late to save Seersha", he said to the grumpy animal.

Sheepig jumped up immediately, putting on a woolly dressing-gown and ice-skates which had been left for him at the bottom of his hammock. The fairy tailor had thought of knitting an entire new wardrobe, including the latest fashions straight off the catwalk for the ungrateful Sheepig.

They let their noses follow the scent of food, and they ended up right back in the banqueting hall they had such fond memories of from the night before.

All the fairies were waiting politely for their guests to arrive, all set to tuck into their frausages, freggs, white frudding, black frudding and froast. There was no stopping Sheepig with so much delicious food to chew on.

He began to stuff his face until there was no room left. His belly was touching the icy floor with the weight of it all. Then, to top it all, he let out a massive burp, so very loud, that everyone in the hall thought it was a thunderstorm, and they dived under the table for cover, almost jumping out of their skin in shock.

"Pardon me for being rude,

It was not me, it was my food,

It just popped up to say hello

And now has all gone down below!" he said in embarrassment, trying to blame anything except his own downright rudeness, as usual.

Luan however, didn't have time to eat, or dive for cover on hearing Sheepig's massive burp. He had more important things on his mind right now.

He headed straight for the mayor's throne, bowing earnestly as he began to speak.

"Thank you so much for your hospitality, Mayor", he said, "but we really must leave you now. We have a very important mission to complete".

"What sort of a mission is it, if you don't mind me asking? I always like to hear of an exciting mission!" asked the mayor, as she sipped a cup of froffee and ate a bowl of snowflakes.

Luan supposed it was safe to tell her. She didn't seem to be a friend of nasty Grandma's, not after the ice-cream incident anyway!

"We're going to Queen Danu the Great's fairy fort!" he announced. "She's my nasty Grandma and she's stolen my little sister and I have to rescue her because it's *my* fault that she stole her in the first place".

A frozen silence descended on the banqueting hall.

Every single jaw in the room dropped on hearing Queen Danu the Great's grandson speak.

Luan took out his mother's map and began to point out his planned route to his captivated audience. "I'm going to cross this mountain range here, I hope it doesn't take too long, and then there should be some sort of a bridge crossing here to ..."

"Ahem". The mayor began to speak.

"You know, young man, there's only *one* safe way into Danu the Great's queendom from here".

"What is it, what's the one safe way?" asked Luan, wondering what was wrong with the way he had suggested.

"Too risky, my boy. Your nasty Grandma's evil spies might capture you, or you might get roasted to death on a spit by the mountain dwairies - they like a good feed of human flesh, they do!" whispered Sheepig, reading the dangers of the route in the mayor's thoughts.

"I guess I'll *definitely* be going the one safe way then!" said Luan, startled by the brutality of Teernoman.

"I promise you that you aren't going to like it", the mayor replied.

"I don't care, I don't care. I'll do *anything* to save my little sister!" he said stubbornly, "and *anything* means *anything!*"

"Have you by any chance noticed that there aren't any children in Ice Town, except my Bubbles, that is?"

Luan hadn't been paying enough attention to notice, but as he looked round the ice hall, he realized she was right. He nodded, wondering what she would say next.

"Queen Danu demands that we send every child over the age of three to an enchanted forest just outside her fort to be educated and trained in her Child Army Camp. We call it the C.A.C. for short", she added.

"The only way for you to reach her queendom safely is if I send you to the Child Army Camp". That didn't sound so bad. Luan could think of worse things, like his encounter with the clairy or the butterbabe or even falling down Fantasy Falls.

"No problemo!" he announced bravely. "I'm sure it's *just* the same as school back at home!"

"Haven't you forgotten something, my boy?" Sheepig piped up, waddling towards him with his heavy belly.

"I don't think so", replied Luan, but he wasn't too sure.

"Well you have, my boy, you certainly have. You know full well that there's no such thing as a fairy *boy*. You'll have to disguise yourself as a fairy *girl* if you want to sneak about Queen Danu's fort unnoticed". Luan looked at the mayor. She was nodding her head in agreement.

"No way! Not a chance!" said Luan. "When I said I'd do *anything* to save Seersha, I meant *anything* except *that*! No way am I dressing up as a girl. There has to be *some* other way", he said, looking around desperately. Everyone in the banqueting hall shook their heads at him.

"But I'm a boy. What would people say if they heard I dressed up as a girl? They'd never let me hear the end of it. I can't do it and *that's that*".

"Nobody is ever going to know. Our lips are sealed, my boy", said Sheepig, pretending to zip his lips together with his trotter. "Besides, your nasty Grandma will *never* notice you if you pretend to be a fairy *girl*. But if she sees a *boy* running round her fort, she'll have you fed to her pet monster Olkas in the blink of an eye".

"Isn't there any other way?" he pleaded. "Sheepig, what about using your magic to get me to nasty Grandma's crystal fort?" He was so desperate that even Sheepig's dodgy magic sounded more appealing to him than having to dress up as a girl. But everyone insisted that there was no other way.

"Guess I've no choice then", Luan said sulkily, "but if you dare tell anyone about this, Sheepig, I'll never speak to you again".

And so it was settled. Luan had to become a fairy girl and as quickly as possible.

The mayor clapped her hands once more, gathering her most skilled workers around her. They began to make a dress and shoes and necklaces and bracelets for Luan under her instruction.

A fairy hairdresser chopped off all of her own long black hair to make a wig for his head. Within seconds all of her own hair had grown back. Luan watched it getting longer and longer until it suddenly stopped, on reaching her ankles. He was horrified at the very idea of even having to wear a wig, but there was no way out. He had agreed to do whatever they told him to do, but only for Seersha's sake.

Sheepig was enjoying himself immensely, chuckling merrily away to himself.

"Don't think I'll be joining you in Queen Danu's fort, my boy. I don't suppose there is any way of making a Sheepig into a fairy girl!" he sniggered.

"Yeah, well, no matter how silly I look, I couldn't possibly look as silly as you did in that green leaf coat of yours!" Luan replied, giving as good as he got.

Sheepig was terribly offended.

"You told me it made me look handsome, Mr Luan. You told me that it brought out the lovely colour of my eyes!"

"Yeah, well I lied to you! Your mind-reading gift isn't so great that it can tell the lies from the truth in someone's mind, can it?!" said Luan cruelly, wanting to hurt Sheepig as much as he had hurt him with his mockery.

"Right, that's it, Mr Luan. If you're going to be rude to me, you can complete your rescue mission all on your own", said a very hurt Sheepig.

"And anyway, let's face it", he said, whispering crossly in Luan's ear, "these people need me here. They couldn't live without me. Just look how happy I make them".

With that, he turned round and waved at everyone who had gone back to eating their breakfast after all the commotion. Hundreds of hands waved straight back at him.

"See what I mean? At least *they* appreciate me for the wonderful Sheepig that I am. I couldn't possibly leave them now. Why, they'd be heartbroken".

Luan was annoyed with himself for getting so cross with Sheepig. He wished he could drag the words he had uttered out of Sheepig's ears, stuff them into his own mouth and swallow them back down to wherever they had come from in the first place, which certainly wasn't his heart. Still, he knew Sheepig wasn't going to change his mind. Sheepig was clearly in his element in the luxury of Ice Town, where he was treated like the King he had always wanted to be.

If Sheepig had decided to abandon him when he needed him most, then there was nothing he could do about it. Besides, he just didn't have time to argue.

"Luan, your new name is Luana", said the mayor, preparing him for Child Army Camp, "and you come from Ice Town. You *love* dolls and *hate* spiders".

Luan cringed at the idea of liking dolls, but he played along with it. The mayor was busy fitting his new wig on his head and zipping him into his dress.

"Just keep quiet in Child Army Camp and you'll be fine. How you find your little sister, I'm afraid, is in your own hands. I can't help you with that".

Luan felt awfully uncomfortable and itchy in his new frilly pink dress. He preferred his pyjamas any day! It was just as well that nobody in BallyBoo could see him now! "What happens in Child Army Camp, is it like school?" Luan inquired.

"Well whatever *school* is, it's a pity they don't teach you some manners there!" Sheepig sneered.

"Now, now, Sheepig, don't be like that", said the mayor of Ice Town. "I'm sure Luan didn't mean what he said. It was just in the heat of the moment".

Luan's head was nodding in agreement.

"And you've been through *so* much together that you really *should* be friends again".

"We'll see, my dear, we'll see", said Sheepig, casting Luan a dirty look as he trotted off amongst his new friends, the people of Ice Town. His stumpy tail was as high in the air as it could reach.

"Don't worry", whispered the mayor to Luan, "I'll use my magical gift to warm his heart, and you'll be the best of friends again before too long".

Luan hoped she was right.

The townsfolk pushed their breakfast aside to accompany 'Luana' to the edge of the town. He said his goodbyes to the mayor and Bubbles but there was no sign of Sheepig at all.

Luan supposed he was either sulking or else had already forgotten about him because he was having so much fun with his new friends. He was very upset that they were of more importance to Sheepig than he was, but he wasn't too surprised by it.

The mayor skated forward as he turned away, leading a snowy white sad-looking one-humped camel behind her. "Just a small token of thanks for returning my little Bubbles", she said, handing him the lead. "Ziphump will carry you safely to the Child Army Camp, just outside Queen Danu the Great's fort". She bowed courteously, retreating back into the middle of the crowd. He could see Bubbles blowing kisses and waving him goodbye. Luan was just hopping up onto Ziphump's back when a snowstorm blew up around him, hiding the townsfolk from view. He was all alone once more. Suddenly he felt very lonely. He missed having Sheepig by his side and calling him 'my boy' in his posh voice all the time. Ziphump certainly didn't seem like the talkative type.

Queen
Danu's
Child
Army
Camp

10

Once again, the weather changed all of a sudden, just as Luan was crossing the border between Ice Town and the queendom of Danu the Great.

He felt so unbearably warm and sweaty that he had to take off his winter woollies, even if it meant that his new frilly dress would be on show for the entire fairy world to see. He couldn't get used to his new hair either, it was making his head terribly itchy.

No birds sang in Danu's queendom. No wind blew. No plants grew. All that could be heard was the weight of Ziphump thumping over the dry sand. Danu's queendom was nothing but a vast arid desert - a desert that made Luan thirst terribly. It was hotter and more stifling than he had ever imagined.

And what made Luan most uncomfortable of all was the fact that Ziphump looked like he was going to have baby camels at any second. His stomach was absolutely huge and swollen-looking and although Luan knew that only female animals could have babies in his own world, that didn't seem to be the case in Teernoman.

"Are you going to have baby camels, Ziphump?" asked Luan politely, not wanting to show how worried he was that *he* would have to deliver them if there was no vet to be found. He had seen a horse having a foal in BallyBoo once and that was enough blood and guts to do him a lifetime! Although, come to think of it, baby camels *could* be fun to play with. Maybe he could teach them how to play football!

Ziphump shook his head sadly in response to Luan's question.

Luan didn't know if he was telling the truth or not, but he decided that if Ziphump wanted to tell him, then he would tell him in his own time.

Ziphump meandered silently across the desert towards the oasis of the Crystal Tower of Light. Luan squinted constantly, the power of the light shining from the tower was hurting his tired eyes. He had to push his wig over his eyes to shade them from its glare.

At long last he was on the final leg of his eventful rescue mission, and he couldn't wait to get it over and done with. Then he could go home and play football with his friends and listen to his mother's bedtime stories again and everything would be back to normal.

The terrible heat was making Luan so excited and nervous as he got closer and closer to his nasty Grandma's fort that his mind was wandering all over the place. One minute he was seeing illusions of himself visiting the Gift Doctor to find out his magical gift, although he had never laid eyes on the woman in his life. The next minute he was seeing an illusion of himself back home in BallyBoo, gobbling up one of his mum's fudge cakes until he felt sick. And then he saw an illusion of himself battling nasty Grandma with all his human strength.

Luckily for Luan Shee, Ziphump's mind most certainly wasn't all over the place. He knew exactly what he was doing and where he was going. He had brought hundreds of children from Ice Town to Child Army Camp over hundreds and hundreds of years. Ever since Queen Danu the Great first built such a camp.

And he brought the children back to their homes again when it was time for their holidays. The change that he saw in them made him ever so sad. They left Ice Town happy and fun-loving and they returned as bullies with broken spirits after being beaten and brainwashed. But there was nothing anyone could do to change the world they lived in. No-one was powerful enough to challenge Queen Danu the Great's rule.

Ziphump, aware that Luan's energy was being zapped by the unbearable heat, stopped off at the only water-well within view and began to sprinkle water all over the boy, bringing him back to his senses. Luan began to ask Ziphump lots and lots of questions as they continued on their journey once more.

"Have you ever seen my Nasty Grandma, Queen Danu the Great?" he asked eagerly.

Ziphump nodded sadly.

"What is she really like? Did she really do all those terrible things that I've heard she's done?"

He nodded sadly again.

"Is she really evil looking? Do I look like her? Does she carry a gun? Can she turn me into a frog?" he asked, bombarding Ziphump with so many questions that he didn't know whether to nod his head or to shake it in response. Eventually he gave up and Luan didn't have any choice but to do the same, even though there were hundreds of questions floating around in his head, just waiting to be asked.

As they left the emptiness of the desert behind them, the volume of traffic dramatically increased. Luan spotted a few fairies travelling along the sandy road, just like himself and Ziphump. Some of them were on zebra-back and horseback, but most of them were on camel-back just like Luan. It seemed to be the most popular mode of transport amongst the fairies. One six-humped camel with lots of fairy children on it sped past them, leaving a cloud of billowing sand in its wake. Luan supposed that it was a family-sized camel, and the children on it were heading to Child Army Camp just like he was.

But there was no point in rushing because they all got caught in a traffic jam anyway, just as Queen Danu the Great's mighty fort became properly visible in the distance. Ziphump stood perfectly still, giving Luan the chance to take in everything around him.

The Crystal Tower of Light was huge and towering, dwarfing every other building for miles around. It was protected by a ring of menacing volcanoes, just like he had imagined them in his mother's stories. Every so often the volcanoes dribbled red-hot lava from their insides as a warning to passersby to stay away if at all possible. It was hideous and beautiful all at once. It took Luan's breath away.

He had never imagined the crystal fairy fort to be so incredibly stunning. Its thick walls were embedded with hundreds of millions of diamonds gleaming through the hazy sunshine.

"There must be an awful lot of toothless fish in the sea!" he said, dazzled by it all.

The sun itself was perched directly above the spiked tip of the Crystal Tower of Light, which made the sun look like it was about to burst open and send rippling waves of light all over the sky, as far as the eye could see.

But there was something horrible hidden deep within the fort's outward beauty. And that something horrible was the evil magician that was Queen Danu the Great. She had made her fairy people's lives miserable in order to make her own so very beautiful.

Just for a split second the idea crossed Luan's mind that maybe, just maybe, he should try to become king of Teernoman after he had saved Seersha. That way he could make sure that nobody was suffering or unhappy, and he could repay the people of Ice Town for their kindness by restoring their sunlight.

Suddenly the traffic jam started to ease, giving Ziphump the chance to press forward once more. He marched sturdily ahead, crossing the heavy glass drawbridge that separated Queen Danu the Great's fort from the mainland. Luan looked into the icy blue water below them, relieved that there was water close at hand if he needed it again. He could see their own reflections alongside that of Queen Danu's mighty fort. He suddenly felt *very* small and *very* insignificant.

The fort entrance, shaped like a lion's open mouth ready to snap, was looming large before their eyes and they were just about to pass through it, when seven fairy guards jumped out of nowhere. They stood in a straight line in front of the entrance, each pointing a huge crystal rifle in the travellers' faces. Luan was frightened out of his wits, but Ziphump just blinked and shook his head sadly. He was used to this sort of hostile treatment in Danu's land.

"What is your name and what is your business, young lady?" they asked at exactly the same time. Luan was startled at being called 'young lady'. He was so busy looking around him that he had forgotten he was supposed to be a girl.

"My name is ... my name is Luana Shee and I'm here to attend Child Army Camp", he stuttered, trying his best to sound like a girl. He giggled a little girly giggle to make himself sound more convincing.

"Very well", they replied, lowering their rifles. "Child Army Camp is in the Enchanted Forest behind the back gate. You can't miss it! By the way, is your camel about to have camel babies?" they asked together, curiously prodding Ziphump's massive belly with the tip of their rifles.

Ziphump shook his head sadly.

Satisfied with his answer, the guards turned round and marched back through the fort entrance, one after the other.

Luan was surprised that they believed that he was a *proper* fairy girl. He hoped that wasn't a sign that he was girly-looking even when he was an ordinary human boy back in BallyBoo! And he was afraid that he might have been right about Ziphump having baby camels now that other people had noticed the size of his tummy too!

They rode around the outside of the fairy fort, until they saw the back gate and beyond it. They could see the Enchanted Forest standing right in front of them.

"It doesn't look half as bad as the clairy's awful forest!" Luan announced to Ziphump.

"But then, I don't suppose you have the faintest idea what I'm talking about, do you, Ziphump?"

Ziphump shook his head slowly and sadly.

"Thought not", said Luan. "It's times like these that I really miss Sheepig's company", he sighed.

Into the Enchanted Forest they went, with Luan not having the slightest idea what to expect. He kept his eyes peeled on the off-chance that he just *might* come across a sweet-tooth tree, and what a welcome treat that would be!

Ziphump obediently followed the forest path, tearing his way through the thickets of brambles and the rustling ivy groping its way towards the sky, choking the very trees that nourished it as it went, until he eventually led Luan into an opening in the middle of the forest.

"Left, left, left, right, left!" shouted a piercing voice behind him.

"Left, left, left, right, left!" repeated lots of childish voices, yelling it as loud as they could.

All of a sudden Ziphump had to jump into a group of trees to let an army of tough little fairy girls march past. They were so busy stamping their feet on the ground and repeating the orders of their captain that they weren't looking where they were going and had very nearly toppled the poor camel over.

Luan couldn't take his eyes off the little fairy girls. They looked just like him in his girly disguise, except that they were much much smaller and tougher. And there were so many of them! He wondered where all the older fairy girls were, though? Did they have to do boring things like school-work when the little fairy girls were being forced to do marching drills? His question was soon to be answered.

Ziphump made his way back onto the path once the child army had passed. He plodded on for a few hundred fairymetres.

They could hear muffled noises coming from just around the corner ...

Luan nearly jumped out of his skin. He had found the older fairy girls alright, but they weren't exactly how he expected them to be!

There they were, in their frilly dresses, hundreds and hundreds of them, playing in the army camp-yard. But they were shooting guns and spitting and sumo-wrestling and kicking each other until they were black and blue. Sumo-wrestling seemed to be a popular sport in Teernoman, but Luan preferred his good old football any day!

He watched one fierce girl, who looked to be the same age as him, as she headbutted the scrawny girl beside her. The scrawny girl, getting her own back, grabbed her attacker by the hair, and tore a lump of it from her scalp with a vicious flick of the wrist.

Soon a huge brawl erupted, with every girl in sight kicking and biting and slashing each other's skin with their razor-sharp finger nails. And the most shocking thing of all was that there was a teacher in a black cloak standing there watching the entire incident, enjoying every minute of it.

They all stopped in their tracks as soon as they noticed the new slightly odd-looking black haired girl on the camel staring at them.

"Silence!" the teacher thundered, kicking the children out of her way as she marched towards Luan. A huge wart was growing on her chin, so huge that it made the rest of her face look tiny compared to it. She looked him up and down, inspecting every little detail. Luan gulped, afraid that she had already guessed his secret.

"Name?!" she yelled in his ear, whipping a notepad out of her cloak to take down his details. He thought his eardrum would burst.

"Luana Shee", he replied in as girlish a voice as he could manage.

"Address?"

"Ice Town".

"Age?"

"Eleven".

"Eleven?!" she boomed. "Eleven?!"

"Why didn't your mother send you here before now? The age of entry to Child Army Camp is three!" she hissed. Luan had to think quickly.

"Well, you see, I'm a bit of a slow learner. In fact I'm not very bright at all so my mother kept me at home ..."

"Silence!" she boomed once more.

Luan's body was shaking under his frilly dress.

"Magical Gift?" she continued.

Luan didn't know whether to answer her or not. One minute she was telling him to be silent, the next she was asking him more questions. He supposed he was doomed either way, and if she wasn't going to murder him herself, then no doubt one of his new classmates would be only too happy to step in!

"Magical Gift?" she repeated in an icy tone of voice. "Shall I spell it out for you? M-A-G-I-C-A-L G-I-F-T!"

"I-I-I'm not quite sure!" he replied. He hung his head, not looking forward to her reaction.

Some of the fairy girls looking on began to snigger at the stupid new girl. How could she possibly be eleven years old and still not know her magical gift? How stupid could she be?!

"I don't suppose you speak Gaelic either then. Oh, maybe I should explain that to you too, considering you're *every bit* as *stupid* as your mother thought! Gaelic is the ancient magical language that we speak when casting spells! If we don't *speak* Gaelic, then the spell just *won't* work!" the teacher explained with sarcasm.

She looked him up and down once more, then sniffed around him suspiciously.

"Go to see the Gift Doctor in Queen Danu the Great's fort, and don't come back until you've been thoroughly examined and have received your Gift Certificate!" she commanded.

Luan didn't have a clue what a Gift Certificate was or what he was supposed to do with it.

"I-I-I don't really know my way round Queen Danu the Great's fort", he stuttered, with as much courage as he could muster up.

"Well, it's just as well your ugly camel *does* then, isn't it!" she said with venom.

She turned her back on Luan and addressed the fairy girls once more.

"Children of Danu, continue your games!" she thundered harshly.

Luan and Ziphump shrugged at one another, turning back in the direction in which they had come, before Warty the teacher got a chance to burst Luan's other eardrum with her screaming.

Back along the forest path they trotted once again, recognizing the familiar scenery. Every so often Luan would catch a glimpse of big yellowy blood-shot eyes staring out at them from the darkness of the forest. But, by the time he had alerted Ziphump, they had always disappeared.

"It's not my imagination, Ziphump, I swear there's something spying on us from the forest!"

Ziphump shook his head sadly and plodded on.

"I swear on my nasty Grandma's future grave if you don't believe me! I wouldn't lie about something like that!" Luan said, frightened. He also thought he could hear the trees whispering to each other as they swayed from side to side in the breeze. It sounded like they were having a game of Chinese whispers, and it was *his* name they were whispering.

"SheeSheeShee!" their rustling leaves whispered to one another. But if Ziphump wouldn't believe him about the eyes spying on them, then he *definitely* wouldn't believe that the trees were talking about him too! Maybe he was just being paranoid.

Ziphump, however, had been shaking his head in his usual sadness, and not in disbelief as Luan had thought. The camel knew perfectly well that there were eyes watching them everywhere they went, even more eyes than Luan had spotted with the limitations of his human eyesight. And he knew that the trees had found out through the grapevine that little black-haired Luana Shee, travelling along the forest path on a camel in her pink frilly dress was none other than Queen Danu the Great's grandson. Of course the trees knew! Of course they were well aware of Luan's rescue mission! And of course they were whispering about it! This forest wasn't called the Enchanted Forest for nothing!

The
Gift
Doctor

11

Luan and Ziphump arrived back to where they had been earlier in the day. They were at the entrance to Queen Danu the Great's fort once more, receiving the *same* treatment from the *same* guards as the last time. The guards jumped out of nowhere. They stood in a straight line in front of the gates, each pointing a crystal rifle in the travellers' faces.

"What is your name and what is your business, young lady?" they all asked at exactly the same time. Luan imagined that they must spend every minute of their free time practising speaking the same words at the same time. How boring a life that must be!

"I'm Luana Shee and I'm here to attend the Gift Doctor".

"Very well", they all replied, lowering their rifles.

"The Gift Doctor's surgery is on the third floor of the first tower on your left. You can't miss it. By the way, is your camel about to have camel babies?" they asked together.

Ziphump shook his head sadly.

"Ha!" whispered Luan to Ziphump, "these guards really do have terrible memories if they can't remember us from earlier, don't they Ziphump?!"

Satisfied with Ziphump's answer to their question, the guards turned round and marched back through the fort gates together.

Ziphump was quick to follow them, before the fort gates closed behind them.

They were in. They were in Queen Danu the Great's crystal fort at long last. Luan wondered whether he should forget about the Gift Doctor altogether and just try to find Seersha straight away. That way he might get out of here and back to BallyBoo much quicker! But would that be the best plan? Or should he at least find out his magical gift first? Maybe it could be a help to him in his rescue mission, although he didn't know how.

He was taking so long to decide his next move that Ziphump had already decided it for him. The camel was already climbing the crystal staircase to the third floor of the first tower on the left, just like the guards at the gate had instructed. Luan clung to his hump, jolting forwards and backwards as Ziphump jumped from one step to the next, with his enormous, bottomless belly hitting the floor each time he moved.

Suddenly a little fairy girl came flying down the stairs.

"Watch out!" she laughed fearlessly, dodging Ziphump, and flying on, out of the tower.

Ziphump politely stepped to the side of the narrow crystal staircase as the girl's grandmother rushed past him trying to catch her little granddaughter, who was now well out of sight.

"Thank you ever so much, dear camel!" the grandmother panted out of breath. "My granddaughter has just been told her magical gift is flying! There'll be no stopping her now!"

"Wait for your old granny, Cleena!" she shouted, charging down the stairs again.

Luan had to laugh. Cleena's grandmother looked so funny trying to catch her! He wondered if his gift would be as exciting as flying. He was getting butterflies in his tummy just thinking about it!

Luan hopped off Ziphump. They were on the third floor of the first tower on the left. And he could see a single door in front of him. It was shaped just like a big pink tongue and on it were the words:

'The Gift Doctor B.U.G., F.A.C.E'.

They were in the right place. Luan knocked on the door. "Yuck! It feels all squishy just like a tongue too!" he said.

"Enter!"

Luan opened the door, followed by a curious Ziphump. He hadn't visited the Gift Doctor's surgery since his youth, and that was a long time ago!

"Name?" demanded a fairy secretary with eyes bulging out through her glasses. She was puffing heartily away at a cigar.

"Luan Shee - or I mean Luana!" Luan spluttered through the tickling smoke, almost giving the game away.

The secretary didn't seem to notice. She just kept on puffing cloud after cloud of thick smoke into the stale air. "Phew! That was a close one!" thought Luan as he tried to wave the lingering smoke away from his face.

"Address?"

"Ice Town, but I'm attending Child Army Camp at the moment, and I'm not quite sure what its address is!" Luan said, doing his best to be helpful.

"Just a moment, please", said the secretary, getting up from her desk and entering another tongue-like door, with 'The Gift Doctor B.U.G., F.A.C.E'. also written on it. Luan wondered what was so special about tongues that the doors were made to look and feel just like them? It seemed just a little bit odd!

Luan and Ziphump took a look around them. They were obviously in the waiting room because there were lots of little fairy girls making a racket, along with an odd zebra and a dwarf-camel for good measure. Luan even spotted a Sheepiggish-looking animal sulking in the corner.

The secretary soon returned, dragging yet another little fairy out of the Gift Doctor's surgery. Everybody in the room turned to stare at her.

But the girl was too busy pulling her tongue out of her mouth to notice them. She pulled and pulled it, and no matter how much she yanked it, it still got longer and longer. She had it wrapped all around her Gift Certificate *and* her body. She had made herself look like a mummy from ancient Egypt before the secretary managed to kick her out of the room.

"Sorry about that!" said the bulging-eyed secretary to Luan and Ziphump, revealing her putrid yellow smoke-coated teeth as she stamped her cigar butt into the carpet. "That young lady's gift has just been diagnosed as an ever-stretching tongue. It will end up running away with her some day if she's not careful! Now, if you'll step this way, the Gift Doctor is awaiting your arrival".

"Children attending Child Army Camp get priority", she announced, before everyone else in the waiting room began to complain that *they* had been waiting longer.

Luan and Ziphump were pushed into the surgery of **'The Gift Doctor B.U.G., F.A.C.E'**.

A middle-aged fairy with grey bug-infested hair greeted them. She swung round in her swivel chair, and jumped up into the air upon their arrival. And, as if having a bug nest on the top of her head wasn't bad enough, a heavy tongue coat complete with buttons and pockets seemed to be growing on her like another layer of skin.

Ziphump made his way quietly to the corner of the room, letting Luan deal with the crazy **'B.U.G., F.A.C.E'** Gift Doctor.

The whole room was like a giant tongue. The carpet and the wallpaper had hundreds of hairy little tongues dotted all over them. There were pictures of signed tongues hanging from the walls, there was a tongue of flames hanging from the ceiling (which was obviously serving as a light bulb to brighten up the room), and there was even a tongue cabinet, with stuffed tongues of all colours and sizes inside it. In the middle of the cabinet there was one big lumpy blue tongue which could have been mistaken for a portion of baked beans gone mouldy. It was *so* disgusting that Luan nearly got sick just looking at it.

"Do you like my tongue museum?" demanded the Gift Doctor, pointing at the tongue cabinet with one hand and scratching her bug-infested head with the other. "Well, do you, do you, do you?"

"Yes, it's very ..."

"That blue tongue belonged to Queen Betty the Brave, Queen Danu the Great's grandmother, oh yes it did, it did, it did!"

"And tell me, don't you think my tongue coat is beautiful, don't you, don't you, don't you?!"

"Yes, it's ..."

"It's not made of *real* fairy tongue, mind you! Hah! I fooled you, didn't I, didn't I, didn't I?!"

"Yes, you d ..."

"It's made from *real* dwairy tongue! Thousands and thousands of dwairy tongues all sewn together! Oh yes it is, it is, it is! Don't look so frightened, young lady, don't you know that dwairy tongue always grows back as soon as it has been snipped off with my tongue scissors! Yes it does, it does, it does!" she said, pointing at a huge ugly silver scissors lying on her desk.

Luan nearly fainted. He hoped that she wouldn't decide to take a snip at his tongue too, because he had never heard of a human tongue growing back before!

"Oh dear, I've forgotten who you are, yes I have, I have, I have!" said the Gift Doctor, jumping up and down in her excitement and sending a swarm of bugs flying in Luan's direction. Luan covered his head with his hands. He felt exhausted just looking at her. Between tongue museums and tongue coats and tongue snipping, he couldn't manage to keep up with her at all!

"I'm Luana Shee, and I'm here to find out my magical gift", said Luan, making sure to say his whole sentence in one breath, before she got a chance to butt in again.

"Oh yes! Silly me! So you are, you are, you are! Stick out your tongue!"

"What?! What do you want to see my tongue for?" Luan said nervously, afraid that his worst fear of getting his tongue cut off to make her another coat was about to come true.

"Go on, give me a little peek, oh do, do, do!"

"Alright", said Luan apprehensively, keeping a close eye on the tongue scissors on her desk. He wondered when she would get around to telling him what his magical gift was.

"Now say 'aaa!' say it, say it, say it!"

He reluctantly stuck out his tongue. "Aaaaaaaaa!"

"Oh my, oh my, oh my!" said the Gift Doctor, examining it closely with a tiny torch, "oh my, oh my, oh my!"

"Why are you saying 'oh my, oh my, oh my' about my tongue?" asked Luan, slightly taken aback. He had a perfectly normal tongue, as far as he was aware.

"Oh my, oh my, oh my!"

"Would you stop saying that and tell me what you're doing!" said a frustrated Luan, grabbing the Gift Doctor's torch and pulling it out of his mouth.

"Oh my, but you're an impatient little girl, but you're an *amazing* little girl too, yes you are, you are, you are!" said the Gift Doctor. Her face had lit up the same colour as her tongue coat in her excitement.

"Well, are you going to tell me *why* I am an *amazing* little girl???"

"Because I've only come across *three* other fairies in my lifetime that have as many secondary gifts as you, yes that's true, that's true, that's true!"

"Hold on a minute, Gift Doctor. Would I be right in thinking that my 'gifts' are written on my tongue and that's why you're so obsessed with tongues?"

The Gift Doctor nodded frantically, dying to reveal the results of her examination. "Can I tell you what your gift is now, can I, can I, can I?" she squealed, jumping up and down more than ever.

Luan would have been far more excited to hear the results if she wasn't so annoying to have to listen to. She was starting to give him a headache. "OK what are my gifts?" he asked nervously.

"Your primary gift is the gift of magical mist, yes it is, it is, it is!" said the Gift Doctor, in a slightly more calm and doctorish tone of voice.

"What exactly is the gift of *magical mist*?" he asked all puzzled. He had expected a gift that he understood the meaning of, at the very least.

"All you have to do to use your gift is suck your left thumb and imagine you're invisible. A magical mist will surround you and make you invisible even to the most magical eye in Teernoman, I lie not, not, not!"

"Cool!" said Luan, already shoving his thumb into his mouth and imagining he was invisible. "Is it working?!"

"Yes it is, it is, it is!" replied the Gift Doctor, going back to her usual silly ways and clapping her hands in glee as she watched the magical mist in front of her.

"That's a really cool gift!" said Luan, taking his thumb out of his mouth in order to speak properly. He became visible once again. Luan could hardly believe that he had *always* had the gift of magical mist within him, but without ever knowing about it. He was going to have some fun with it when he got back to BallyBoo, *and* more importantly, it was going to be a great help to him in rescuing Seersha from nasty Grandma.

"I bet you would like to hear more, wouldn't you, wouldn't you, wouldn't you?" said the Gift Doctor eagerly.

"Yes I would like to hear more, as long as you stop doing that annoying thing with your words!" replied Luan. He was being honest if nothing else!

"Oh!" said the Gift doctor, "very well then". She sounded a little hurt. "Like I said, I've only come across three fairies in my lifetime that have as many secondary gifts as you young lady, and they just happen to be the *entire* Royal Family - Queen Danu the

Great herself, her daughter and her granddaughter whom I examined just last week".

Luan bit his lip. "What does a secondary gift mean?" he asked, changing the topic of conversation in the hope that she wouldn't realize that *he too* was a member of the Royal Family. He was dying to ask her how little Seersha was, and where exactly nasty Grandma was keeping her prisoner, but he daren't!

"A secondary gift is not your main gift, but you can use it all the same. It makes you incredibly powerful. There's a book, now what's the name of it again, ah yes, *The Glorious Book of Change* that's it! Only the very gifted few are powerful enough to use it, and you just happen to be one of those very gifted few, young lady. I'll have to tell the Queen of this startling revelation, she shall want to meet you".

"No, no, no!" said Luan, starting to sound like the Gift Doctor herself. "Why don't you just give me my certificate for Child Army Camp, and I'll arrange to meet the Queen myself! You've *so* many patients waiting to see you that you couldn't possibly afford the time!" It was the only idea that came into his mind.

"Oh, I must tell the Queen about my exciting discovery straight away, I must, I must, I must!" she exclaimed, going back to her old habit of repeating herself over and over again.

Luan was getting frantic. This crazy Gift Doctor could ruin absolutely everything if he wasn't careful.

"Tell you what, Gift Doctor, if you let me tell the Queen myself, I'll donate my tongue to your tongue museum when I die. How does that sound?"

"Ooooh! You know what makes me a happy Gift Doctor, don't you, you clever young lady, don't you, don't you, don't you?!" she said, before pausing for a moment of reflection. "But as long as there is eternal life in this land, you won't ever die, no you won't, you won't, you won't!" she added somewhat suspiciously.

Luan hadn't thought of that. He felt like hitting his head off a brick wall for saying something that sounded so foolish to her ears. "Well I have no intention of living forever", he announced, doing his best to cover his tracks.

"And even if I do decide to live forever, once I have eaten enough food to last me a lifetime and spoken enough words to last me a lifetime, I won't need my tongue anymore, so I'll give it to you then".

With that the Gift Doctor swivelled round to her tongue-shaped desk in her chair, grabbing a certificate from the middle of a big pile. The whole pile came crashing down around her and Luan set about picking them up as she filled in his Gift Certificate. She had seemed satisfied with his answer, but he couldn't be sure. All he could do was hope that she wouldn't alert nasty Grandma.

And if she did alert her, Luan hoped that his nasty Grandma wouldn't murder him. He hated the thought of his tongue being cut out of his mouth with a tongue scissors. And he hated even more the thought of it being stored in a horrible tongue museum for ever and ever.

"Now, young lady, I hope you use your gifts wisely, yes I do, I do, I do!" she said, shaking Luan's hand and giving him his Gift Certificate. "Stick out your tongue for the camera! Do it, do it, do it!" The flash of a camera lit up the entire room, taking Luan completely by surprise. The flashing light must have given the bugs in the Gift Doctor's hair an unexpected shock too because they began to topple out of her hair and fall to their death on the tongue carpet far below, until the carpet was a black bug-graveyard. The Gift Docter, oblivious to the bugs spiralling downwards like confetti around her, became crazier than ever and quickly produced a photograph of herself and Luan with their pink tongues hanging out just like Spike the dog's tongue.

"That's for you, young lady, just to remember your first ever trip to the Gift Doctor. It's a very special day for you, yes it is, it is, it is!"

"Thanks, Gift Doctor!" he said, grabbing his photograph and Gift Certificate and getting out of her surgery as quickly as possible, with Ziphump hot on his heels. The Gift Doctor was *so* annoying that he couldn't stick her for another minute. But at least she had diagnosed his gift, and had agreed not to tell nasty Grandma about him; that, at least was a bonus! Luan hopped up on Ziphump's back once again, as they left the third floor of the first tower on the left. He unscrolled his Gift Certificate, looking at it proudly. He read it aloud:

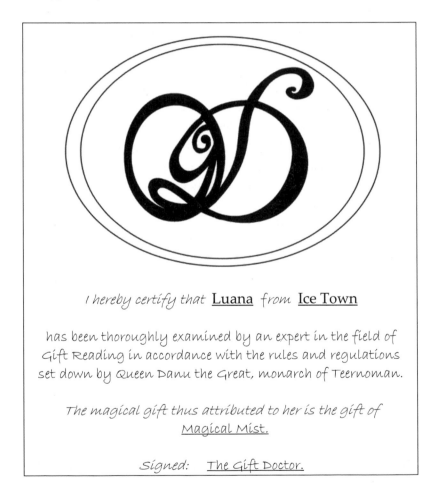

I hereby certify that **Luana** *from* **Ice Town**

has been thoroughly examined by an expert in the field of Gift Reading in accordance with the rules and regulations set down by Queen Danu the Great, monarch of Teernoman.

The magical gift thus attributed to her is the gift of Magical Mist.

Signed: The Gift Doctor.

"Ha! Who would have thought it! Me with a magical gift!" said Luan as they trotted back through the gates of Queen Danu's fort once again. "Only a week ago I thought I was exactly the same as every other human boy in the world and look at me now! How quickly things can change!"

It was only as they left the fort behind them that Luan realized he should have been keeping an eye out for Seersha all the time he was busy thinking about himself and his gift. Whether he liked it or not, he was going to have to find her before the night was over, but he'd better go back to Child Army Camp with his certificate first, before someone there realized that he hadn't returned and raised the alarm.

Luan and Ziphump didn't pay much attention to the fairies passing them by on their way back to the Enchanted Forest. They had seen plenty of fairies before now and chances were they would see plenty again before their journey's end.

But there was one beautiful fairy girl, only slightly older than Luan, that grabbed Luan's attention. He had barely got a glimpse of her as she bolted past him on her snow white horse, but there was something different about her that drew him towards her. He felt like she had warmed his heart as she passed him by. It sounded silly, but no matter how hard he tried to concentrate on his rescue mission or his magical gift, the feeling of warmth didn't go away. He put his hand on his chest just to be sure that she hadn't done something strange to his heart - you never knew what kind of strange magical gifts people had in Teernoman!

Sure enough, the warmth he felt wasn't a figment of his imagination at all. It was because of his mother's locket of remembrance, which was all lit up and blazing like a burning ball of fire, next to his heart. Luan got an awful shock. He pulled it off in panic, juggling it from hand to hand as he did his best to blow out the fire.

But he soon realized that the fire wasn't burning him at all. It didn't even mark his skin and he didn't feel any pain whatsoever.

"That's weird, what's the point of a fire that doesn't burn?" he asked Ziphump, forgetting how unlikely he was to get a response from the camel. He threw the ball of fire onto the forest floor, and the camel obliged him by stamping on it until the blaze died down. A single puff of smoke rose high into the evening sky.

Luan picked up the locket to examine it closely. It was still intact, with a reddish-orange glow emanating from it. He ran his fingers over the locket of remembrance. It seemed to be ever so slightly different. He ran his fingers over it once again just to make sure it was alright.

"Look, Ziphump, there's a message engraved on it!" he exclaimed in utter surprise. "The fairy girl on the white horse must have sent it to me!" He couldn't believe his eyes. Just when he thought everything was starting to make a little sense to him in Teernoman, yet another strange thing had happened to him. He was squinting with the effort of reading the engraved message with its tiny lettering. He read it quietly and slowly to himself, afraid that the trees would hear.

"Luan Shee, you can't fool me,
You've got your mother's eyes.
Danu's spies have tracked you down,
Despite your cunning disguise.

Go now to Child Army Camp,
And make sure you do not stray,
Tonight when the stars get bright,
I'll whisk you and Seersha away.

Be prepared, your time has come,
Queen Danu has planned your end,
Olkas, her pet, awaits you,
But fear not, I am your friend".

Luan was more terrified than ever before.

"Nasty Grandma has found me out! And her pet Olkas awaits me! What am I going to do?!" He read the message again. It wasn't signed by anyone. How did he know that the fairy who wrote it wasn't a spy of his nasty Grandma's, trying to lure him into a trap? He wished Sheepig was with him to read the mind of the fairy girl on the white horse. At least that way he would know if she was a spy or not.

But hold on, if she was a spy, and she did try to imprison him or kill him that night, when the stars get bright, then he could use his gift of magical mist to escape from her sight! Brilliant! He had nothing to worry about then. That took a weight off his shoulders.

Luan and Ziphump arrived back at Child Army Camp just as night was falling. A mist covered the treetops like a cozy blanket and all the children were busy gathering whatever bits of firewood they could find for the campfire. But they were really more interested in catching glow-worms and squelching them mercilessly into the ground with their steel-capped boots, leaving a splatter of mushy glow-worm guts on the forest floor behind them.

Luan spotted the dark figure of Warty the teacher, and made straight for her with his new Gift Certificate.

"Give me that!" she bellowed, swiping the certificate from Luan's trembling fingers and studying it with intense interest. Then she tore it up.

"What are you doing?" wailed Luan before he could stop himself.

"What do you think I'm doing, you stupid girl? Now leave your ugly stinking camel in the stables and be back here before night-time magic lessons begin!"

Luan obediently followed her orders. He hadn't the faintest idea why she had torn up his Gift Certificate after all the trouble he had gone to in order to get it. Still, as long as he knew what his gift was and knew how to use it, that was the most important thing.

The stable was quite a distance away, and when they got there, a dirty and smelly little room greeted them, just as dirty and smelly as the yard the fairy children were playing their so-called 'games' in much earlier that day.

Luan jumped off Ziphump and patted him on the back. He was just about to walk out the stable door when Ziphump spoke for the first time. His words were slow and sad.

"Aaaren't yoouu gooiing tooo uuunziiip mmmy huuump", he said, pronouncing every syllable. Luan turned on his heel, taking a good long look at the camel.

"I never knew it was possible to unzip your hump!" he eventually said, "and what's more, when did you learn to speak?!"

"Ooone woouuld neeever guueess thaaat aaa caaamel caaalled Ziiiphuuump woouuld haaave aaa huuump tooo uuunziiip", he replied, ignoring the second part of Luan's question. His voice sounded so sad and depressed that, if Luan hadn't been so surprised to hear about his unzippable hump, it would have made him start to cry on the spot.

"Would you like me to unzip your hump for you then?" Luan asked, trying to cheer him up a bit by offering to help him.

"Dooeessn't booother meee, buuut yoouu miiight liiike tooo knooow whyy III looooook liiike III'm aaaboouut tooo haaave baaaby caaamels", came the reply. Luan was getting edgy. Of course he wanted to know why Ziphump looked like he was going to have baby camels, but he would be in trouble with Warty the teacher for being late if Ziphump kept this up, and he had already got off to a bad start with her by the looks of things.

"Ooof coouurse, whaaats iiin mmy huuump miiight beee ooof mooore iiinteeereeest tooo yoouu thaaan iiit iiis tooo meee", he sniffed after a long pause.

"There there, Ziphump!" whispered Luan reassuringly, while he himself was getting more edgy by the minute. He looked quickly over his shoulder in case anyone was spying on them.

"I'm going to unzip your hump for you. And please cheer up, things aren't really as bad as they might seem. My mother always tells me that things are never as bad as they seem, and she should know!"

With that, Luan unzipped the entire hump, watching it fall to the ground. Not alone had Ziphump got a hump-hole, but his entire insides were hollow and empty too! Luan stuck his hand into the hump-hole, standing on his tip-toes as he fumbled about in it. He stuck the other hand in too, pulling out one thing after another.

First came a lunchbox of half-eaten friscuits and frakes. Luan wondered why the people of Ice Town would pack half-eaten food for him. It seemed a bit strange. And it certainly wasn't the weight of a half-eaten lunchbox of friscuits and frakes that made Ziphump look as if he was about to have baby camels, so there must still be something a lot heavier inside the hump-hole.

"It was thoughtful of your people to send me any sort of food, half-eaten or not", he said to Ziphump, giving him a hug in gratitude. Ziphump smiled for the first time ever. It looked like a frown at first, but then his face lit up and he showed off two rows of dazzling white teeth.

Luan kept on rummaging in the hump-hole. Next came - a map of nasty Grandma's fairy fort, and it was up-to-date too!

"That'll come in handy for my rescue mission", he said, tucking it under his dress for safety. He started to pull out something else from the hump-hole.

He was so excited that it reminded him of opening his presents on Christmas morning back at home.

It felt like the shape of a watch.

"Oh brilliant, brilliant!" he exclaimed in excitement, "a home detector to help me and Seersha escape back to BallyBoo without getting lost! Brilliant!" He tied it to his wrist at once and pulled the sleeve of his dress down over it in case anyone would notice it.

He delved his hands into the hump-hole for the last time. He could feel something big and soft and squishy but no matter how hard he tried to lift it out, he couldn't manage. Whatever it was, it was what was causing Ziphump to have the enormous tummy...

"Stop poking me, my boy, do you not know how annoying it is to be poked when you're trying to take a nap?!"

Luan thought he was hearing things.

He poked the big, soft, squishy thing again just to be certain.

"Stop it I said. Honestly, Mr Luan, you really seem to know how to get up a Sheepig's snout!"

As Luan heard those words, up popped Sheepig's reddening face out of the hump-hole, as large and as full of life as ever. And there were friscuit and frake crumbs all over his face. Now the mystery of the half-eaten friscuits and frakes made perfect sense to him. However, Luan was *sure* he was dreaming! He rubbed his eyes and took another look.

He wasn't dreaming at all.

"But you're supposed to be back in Ice Town!" Luan exclaimed, finding it hard to contain his happiness on seeing his old friend.

"Yes, I was rather tempted to stay there, my boy, wonderful place! But we had a deal, remember? I said I would help you on your rescue mission if you would help me to return to the Sty. And a deal is a deal. Anyway, I knew deep down that you could never survive without me, so I decided to travel in Ziphump's hump-hole. That way I could have a nice long nap before we started our rescue mission. Now where are we?" he asked, looking all around him. "I haven't missed all the fun, have I?"

Good old Sheepig, he hadn't changed one bit!

"Sssh! Sheepig, keep your voice down, or we'll get caught!" said Luan, looking around again to make sure nobody was around to eavesdrop.

"You've missed so much, Sheepig! I've been to the Gift Doctor in nasty Grandma's fort and I've found out my magical gift and I've got a message from some fairy girl who says she's my friend but I don't know if she is or not, and she says some guy called Olkas is waiting for me and and and ..."

"Slow down, my boy, now first things first. Enlighten me as to what your magical gift may be".

"Magical mist!"

"*Magical mist?* Well, my boy, you're on to a good thing there, might I say!" said Sheepig clapping Luan on the back.

'Oh, Sheepig, I've got to go or I'll be in trouble!" said Luan, forgetting in his excitement that he was supposed to be back with the rest of the children attending Child Army Camp long ago.

"It's too dangerous for you to come with me!"

"Too dangerous for me? Why, *nothing* is too dangerous for a Sheepig like me, my boy. Tell you what, I'll just nibble on some food then go back to sleep in Ziphump's hump-hole and you can wake me when you need me, if that makes you feel better. As long as that is alright with you, Ziphump?"

"Ceeertaaainly mmmy frieeend!" said Ziphump, finding his new smile once more. It was such a pleasant change.

That sounded like the best idea to Luan. That way Sheepig would be out of harm's way, because if Warty the teacher found a Sheepig wandering round Child Army Camp, who knows what she would do to him!

Luan shoved Sheepig back into the hump-hole and zipped the hump back on. Ziphump's tummy dropped to the ground with Sheepig's weight once more, and Luan wondered how the camel had possibly managed to carry them both.

Then he left the stable, making his way back to Child Army Camp, following the light of the burning campfire, which by now was blazing through the darkness.

Luan fixed his wig firmly on his head and crept silently into the circle of fairy children sitting cross-legged around the campfire. Nobody noticed his arrival except the two girls who had to push over to make space for him to sit down. He breathed a sigh of relief. He had hoped that the children would be having a singsong or else toasting marshmallows at the fire, but no such luck.

A complicated magic lesson was underway, and Luan didn't have a clue what was happening. Warty the teacher was chanting in what must have been the magical ancient Gaelic language because Luan didn't understand a word of it. He just stared deep into the warm crackling fire and thought about the happiness he felt on seeing Sheepig again. He began to plan the long night ahead of him, letting his imagination run wild.

"You! Luana Shee!" Warty screamed, bringing Luan back to his senses with a jump. She started belting him over the head with a magic wand.

"What magic do you know?" she demanded to know.

"I don't know any at all", he replied meekly, squinting in order to see her face through the shadows.

"No magic at all!" she thundered, belting him again. He hated the way she always seemed to be picking on him, even though it was only his first day. It was just as well that he didn't plan on staying long!

"Weren't you listening to what I've been teaching you for the last hour? Piansa Toun, tell this idiot the rules of magic!" she commanded, waving her wand at a snooty little girl of about six, who was busy warming her hands at the fire.

Piansa Toun stood up and started to swoop and prance around the campfire. She was wearing a pure white dress and reminded Luan of a ghost performing some sort of magic ritual.

"There are three rules of magic", she repeated in an annoying voice, that wasn't remotely ghost-like, mind you. She rattled them off by heart as she pranced about.

"**Number One:** Never try to trick Queen Danu the Great by using magic, for Her Highness is the most magical fairy of all and will kill you if you do".

"**Number Two:** You may use magic to kill *any* enemy of Queen Danu's that you may come across in your life".

"**Number Three:** Only direct descendants of Her Highness may use the magic of *The Glorious Book of Change*, and because none of us *are* her direct descendants, we are forbidden to do so much as speak of it".

The rest of the children, who had been silent up until now, started booing and wolf-whistling and stamping their feet as soon as she had finished. Luan decided that Piansa Toun mustn't be the most popular girl in Child Army Camp at all!

But he *was* intrigued by what Piansa Toun had said all the same. *The Glorious Book of Change.* That was the same book the Gift Doctor had told him about, he was sure of it. The book that only the gifted few were powerful enough to use, she had said. And he knew that he was one of those few.

He said the words over and over in his head. It sounded like a very exciting book, *very* exciting and a little bit scary too! He wondered what was in it, and why only he, nasty Grandma, his mother and his little sister could use it.

"Let's show this Luana Shee idiot the simplest magic spell in the world then, seeing as she isn't very bright", Warty the teacher sneered, picking on Luan as usual, but Luan was staring deep into the fire once more and heard nothing of what was going on around him.

"Bedtime! Go to your tents!" was the next thing that Luan heard. He blindly followed the path the rest of the children were taking through the Enchanted Forest, lit only by glow-worms crawling along the forest floor and the odd lightning bug whooshing by. He hoped that they knew where they were going. They were pushing and shoving and mocking Piansa Toun's prancing around the campfire. He kept close behind them, but not too close. He didn't want them to start mocking him next. He kept his eyes wide open at all times just in case nasty Grandma's spies were waiting behind some tree to snatch him...

The children came to a wooded hillside, dotted with rows and rows of tents. Luan kept on following the children, until one by one they disappeared into their own tents. He wondered how they could remember which was theirs because they all looked exactly the same to him.

It was then that he noticed tiny little name-tags glowing in the dark at the entrance to each tent. They were barely noticeable to the human eye.

He looked long and hard as he passed each and every tent, searching for his glowing name. Some children stuck their legs out of their tents to trip him up as he went by. They sniggered quietly to themselves each time he fell flat on his face, until they grew tired of the same old joke being played over and over again. But Luan didn't care. He was too busy searching row after row of tents for his name, until finally, there it was. It was exactly what he was looking for. The name 'Luana Shee' glowing through the darkness and staring him in the face.

Luan crawled into his tent. It was all hot and stuffy. Now, at least, he had a little bit of time to himself, to study his map of nasty Grandma's fort and plan his rescue mission, hopefully avoiding nasty Grandma's pet Olkas. *He* didn't sound too friendly.

Luan sat upright in his little tent, learning every little nook and cranny in Queen Danu's fort off by heart from his new map.

There were only a few little problems left for him to iron out before he rescued Seersha. First of all, he would have to find out where exactly she was being held prisoner. Then he would have to find some secret way out of the fort where nobody could catch them. And the words that the Gift Doctor and Piansa Toun had uttered - *The Glorious Book of Change* - were still at the back of his mind. Something deep inside him, although he had no idea what, made him want to see that book almost as much as he wanted to see Seersha.

Still, he would have to wait until the stars got bright to see if the fairy girl on the white horse would turn up. But how would she know where to find him? Even if she *was* a friend like she said, and not a spy, it would take her the whole night to find Luan's tent amongst all the other tents.

Luan waited and waited, peeking out through his tent to watch the stars getting brighter and brighter and starting to twinkle in the still night sky. Then he raised his thumb to his mouth and imagined he was invisible just like the Gift Doctor had told him to. His magical gift worked straight away, and all that would have been seen if anyone looked into Luana Shee's tent just then, was a wispy steaming magical mist. He was using it to hide himself from the view of the fairy girl, if she ever showed up.

Warty the teacher was pacing up and down the rows of tents. She knew there was something not quite right about this Luana Shee child, but exactly what was not quite right about her. Warty just couldn't decide. She smelt a little bit odd and she looked a little bit odd, but so did half the children in Child Army Camp! Still, she would keep a close eye on her over the next few days, deciding whether or not to inform Queen Danu the Great about this suspicious new fairy girl with the gift of magical mist.

The fairy girl that Luan had seen on the white horse was watching Warty the teacher very carefully from the shadow of the trees. She waited for Warty to pace past Luan's tent with her back to her so that she wouldn't be seen. She was without her white horse this time and she crept silently through the rows of tents, without making a sound. She found Luan's tent without any bother and poked her beautiful head through its entrance. The wispy steaming mist, the product of Luan's newfound magical gift, greeted her.

"Luan, it's me! Cara Shee! Your mother's best friend!" she whispered, knowing perfectly well what Luan was up to.

Olkas and the Crystal Tower of Light

12

Luan's jaw dropped in surprise and his thumb slid out of his mouth. He immediately returned to his normal girlish form.

"Cara Shee!" he almost yelled, if she hadn't put her hand over his mouth in time to quiet him. "But you're supposed to be as old as my mother!" he whispered.

"I am as old as your mother, but time passes much more slowly in Teernoman, that's why I look younger than your mother", she replied.

"How did you know it was me?" he asked, puzzled. He was relieved beyond belief that he certainly wasn't dealing with one of nasty Grandma's spies.

"Your mother has been sending me starletters all along, so I've been keeping an eye out for you. You couldn't fool me with that silly costume of yours, whatever about fooling old Warty the teacher. I know a human boy when I see one!" she said laughing. "And as for calling yourself Luana Shee", she continued, "now that's what I call a dead giveaway!"

Luan was glad she had found him. It was good to have someone around who knew every inch of the fort.

"Oh, before I forget, your mother sent you this", she whispered as she produced a shiny golden parcel from under her purple cloak. Luan ran his fingers over the smooth surface in surprise, wondering what exactly it was. It had the texture and the colour of a star, but it was much thicker and heavier.

"Aren't you going to open your starparcel?" asked Cara, more excited than Luan as to what it was his mother had sent him.

"Starparcel?!" exclaimed Luan, "well, I suppose that does make sense, come to think of it", he mused as he fumbled with the thick star wrapping. He peeled off layer after layer until he was left with nothing but a little mirror, the size of the palm of his hand. "That's my dad's old shaving mirror!" he announced, wondering what had possessed his mother to send him such a useless present. He looked to see if she had sent any sort of a hidden message along with it, but to no avail. There was nothing there at all.

"What is it?" asked Cara, studying it with such interest that Luan began to wonder whether or not she had ever seen a mirror before.

"It's a mirror! It shows your reflection, see?" he replied, giving Cara the best demonstration he could through the darkness.

"Ooh! Is that really me in the 'mirror' as you call it? But how can there be another me staring back at me when I'm the only me?" came her confused response. "How unusual!" she added after a moment's thought. Luan didn't have time just then to explain to her how the mirror worked.

"I don't suppose you know why my mother sent it to me, do you, Cara?" he asked doubtfully.

Cara shook her head. "Maybe it's got something to do with one of your secondary gifts. Maybe your instincts will tell you when to use it, I really don't know", she said, shrugging.

Luan decided there wasn't a lot he could do about his father's mirror right now, except to put it in his pocket. No doubt he would find some important use for it later or else his mother would never have gone to the trouble of sending it to him in the first place.

"Do you know where my little sister is?" he whispered in her ear, showing her the map that the people of Ice Town had put in

Ziphump's hump-hole. She pointed to the Crystal Tower of Light on the map.

"She's locked up at the top of it along with the rest of Queen Danu's most precious possessions!"

"Can we go there now, right now?" he pleaded, but she shook her head.

"Queen Danu's pet monster, Olkas, is guarding it as we speak. He always falls asleep at the crack of dawn, when the sun rises to the top of the crystal tower, and Queen Danu wakes up minutes after he falls asleep, so we've got to rescue Seersha during that time".

It sounded like Cara Shee had been doing some very good spying and eavesdropping to find out such important information.

'All we can do right now is sit and wait for Warty to go to bed, and then we'll be off to complete your rescue mission", she added.

So there they sat in silence, peeking through the tent at Warty doing her rounds, over and over again. They listened to the snoring and sighing and crying of the sleeping children in the tents around them.

Luan's mind was racing. He was imagining the heroic deeds he was about to accomplish. He would chop nasty Grandma's head off, and free the people of Teernoman. He would declare it Christmas all year round and there would be no more Child Army Camp or anything like it; he might even make Sheepig king of the Sty ... He suddenly felt the urge to ask Cara Shee something that had been pushed to the back of his mind.

"Do you know what *The Glorious Book of Change* is, Cara, or even where I could find it?"

"Sssh! Don't talk so loud or someone will hear us! There are spies everywhere in this Enchanted Forest, even some of the children are spies!"

That made Luan feel very uneasy, but he persisted in asking his question anyway, he *had* to know.

"Well, do you know anything about *The Glorious Book of Change?*" he persisted, more quietly this time.

"Not a lot", she said, "but I do know that it's supposed to be the most magical book ever written. Its magic can change the world, but only if it's used by a descendant of the Queen. I've heard that it is kept in the Crystal Tower of Light too, but I can't be sure of it".

The more Luan heard about this *Glorious Book of Change*, the more he wanted to get his hands on it. He could use it to fix *every* single bad thing that his nasty Grandma had ever done.

But first things first, he had to think about rescuing Seersha.

The night passed slowly and the pair in the tent took their time in finalizing their rescue plan. Warty was still pacing up and down the rows of tents.

They talked their plan over again and again, so that nothing could possibly go wrong.

Cara would keep watch while Luan entered the Crystal Tower of Light. He would climb the steps to the top of it, grab Seersha and get out of there as quickly as possible, before Queen Danu awoke, and he would be all tucked up in bed in BallyBoo by the time anyone would notice that Seersha Shee was missing. After all his trouble finding his way to Teernoman and then to Queen Danu the Great's fairy fort, this part of his adventure sounded like it was going to be the easiest part of all.

"But what about the guards at the fort gates?" asked Luan. "How will we get past them?"

"I've already dealt with them!" said Cara mischievously, "come on, the coast is clear, it's time to go!"

They were all set. It was time for action. Luan took a deep breath as Cara crawled out of the tent and tip-toed through the darkness. He was right behind her. They slipped silently through the Enchanted Forest to the stables where Cara had left her white horse alongside Ziphump.

Luan did his best to wake the snoring Sheepig in Ziphump's hump-hole, but he was in such a deep sleep that neither he nor Cara could manage to wake him with all the poking in the world. Still, they could do without him now. Luan and Cara mounted her horse, Lightning, who darted through the darkness, watching out for the shadows of sneaky spies lurking round every corner.

They galloped on through the darkness, whizzing through the forest and past the guards lying fast asleep in front of the entrance to nasty Grandma's fairy fort. They were all snoring loudly. They sounded like a brass band playing by starlight.

"What did you do to them, Cara?" asked Luan, laughing at the funny noise they were making.

Cara just winked and smiled in reply, tossing her mane of long blonde hair back in the wind.

They galloped on through Queen Danu the Great's fort until they were standing directly opposite the mighty Crystal Tower of Light. Even in the darkness it shimmered and glittered, taking Luan's breath away once more.

Luan recognized his surroundings from his new map - everything was exactly as he expected it to be and as beautiful as his mother had always told him it was. Everything was made from crystal.

"I'll be waiting here for you when you've got Seersha", Cara whispered, helping Luan to the ground. "If Queen Danu appears earlier than expected I'll whistle to let you know. Good luck, Luan!"

"Oh, and one last thing", she added "watch out for Olkas's poisonous eye - if he squirts poison from it at you, you're a dead man!"

Luan didn't want to hear that, but he supposed it might be a useful thing to know. Off he went, all alone, to the door of the Crystal Tower of Light. He looked back at Cara for moral support. She was hiding in the shadows at the other side of the courtyard.

Luan didn't know what to expect. He knew that nasty Grandma's pet Olkas always fell asleep at the crack of dawn. Only then would he make his move.

In the meantime, he crouched outside the door of the Crystal Tower, hoping that nobody was awake to spot him.

He waited and waited but there was no sign of the dawn. He began to worry. What if the sun didn't come out in time? Or what if it did come out, but without warning, and Queen Danu's guards spotted him? What then? No, on second thoughts, he decided he would have to act straight away, whether Olkas slept or not.

He tip-toed up to the crystal door. It was gigantic. He had never seen a door so big! He opened it gently and carefully, making sure that it didn't creak. He was in.

The inside of the tower had ceilings so high that he couldn't see the top of them. It glistened and sparkled even more than the outside did, although he wouldn't have thought that possible. But there was an eerie silence that made him feel awfully uneasy.

Luan knew he didn't have time to look around. If Olkas wasn't there, as he had expected him to be, well that was just an added bonus!

He was a man with a mission. He spotted the stairs leading to the room at the top of the tower where little Seersha was hidden. Off he sped across the room to get to it. He had jumped up about five steps when he felt something land on his shoulder with such force that he put his hands over his head to protect himself, thinking the roof was collapsing on top of him. He tried to shake off whatever it was, but it wouldn't budge.

"It must be Olkas!" he said, bracing himself to turn round and face his nasty Grandma's pet monster.

He turned round and looked up and up. His face turned whiter than a ghost.

He was lifted straight up off the ground by the enormous hand that had landed on his shoulder. His little feet dangled in mid-air. An equally enormous blue eye with lashes the length of windscreen wipers was peering at him in surprise. The eye blinked and Luan had to dodge the lashes, which nearly gave him a terrible whack.

"You-you-you must be Olkas", stuttered Luan, struggling to free himself from the monster's grip. "It's a pleasure to meet you!" He couldn't think of anything better to say under the circumstances.

Olkas didn't reply. He just stood there looking stupid and squeezing Luan all the more.

"Has anyone ever told you how beautiful your eyes are?", Luan said, deciding that flattery was the best way to get in this stupid monster's good books. Olkas smiled and loosened his grip.

"I would love to have eyes like yours, and I'm sure every other fairy girl in Teernoman would too!"

"Yes! It's working! It's working!" thought Luan to himself, delighted with his simple strategy.

Olkas was delighted with his compliments. Nobody had ever said such kind things to him before! He was just about to set Luan down on the ground in gratitude for his kindness when Sheepig turned up out of the blue, as he had a habit of doing.

"Never fear, my boy, I'm here to save you!" came Sheepig's squeal, echoing through the room, as his head popped out of the humpless Ziphump's hump-hole.

A crunching sound and a thundering yelp from Olkas followed this. Sheepig had taken a bite of one of Olkas's dirty big toes.

Olkas grew more angry the more the little Sheepig bit him, and with one almighty creak, he flapped open his other eye, his poisonous eye, just like a blind, spraying its poisonous fluid all over the ground, trying to kill Sheepig.

"Can't catch me, big fellow!" Sheepig teased, directing Ziphump to prance around Olkas's feet just to annoy the monster even more. Olkas was furious. He raised his free hand to his mouth and blew a shrill whistle through his fingers.

"Can't deafen me either, big fellow!" Sheepig laughed, biting another toe and then bursting into one of his many inappropriate songs:

"You can kill a fairy,
You can kill a tree,
You can kill a dwairy,
But you can't kill me!

You can kill a teacher,
You can kill a flea,
You can kill all creatures,
But you can't kill me!"

He was really enjoying himself, but Luan wished that he would just shut up and go away. Things had been starting to go well before he had turned up!

Without warning, a circle of mini-Olkases had surrounded the animal, flapping their eyes open just like their father had done and trying to squirt poison all over him. Sheepig ducked back into Ziphump's hump-hole for cover, leaving Ziphump in the line of fire. The mini-Olkases squirted Ziphump without mercy and within seconds the poor camel fell to the ground motionless.

Luan watched on, terrified, horrified, devastated that the camel had lost his life trying to save him.

Suddenly Olkas's eyes snapped shut and so did the eyes of each and every mini-Olkas. They all stood still as statues. And they all started to snore standing up. The break of dawn had arrived.

"Perfect timing!" thought Luan, hardly believing his luck. He squeezed his body out of Olkas's tightly clenched fist, abseiling down to the ground. He began to climb the stairs again.

Hopefully this time he would make it to the top of the Crystal Tower, where Seersha was being kept prisoner, without any trouble.

Sheepig's head popped cautiously out of Ziphump's hump-hole after the danger was all over, not looking half as brash and sure of himself as he did when he was teasing Olkas. He inspected his woolly coat for any traces of poison and then he looked guiltily at the camel, but was quick to leave his guilt behind him in order to catch up with Luan.

The stairs spiralled up and up and there seemed to be no end to them. Luan's breath grew heavier and he heaved and stumbled the nearer he came to the top.

And then he was there.

He fell through the glass door at the entrance of the room, not knowing that there was a door there at all. It smashed into little pieces all over the floor and cut him to shreds, but he didn't even notice.

He spotted a little crystal cradle rocking gently at the other side of the room. He ran to it faster than he had ever run before. And there she was, at last he could see her again, little Seersha Shee, just as he had remembered her. She hadn't changed one bit to look at, although he didn't know if nasty Grandma had brainwashed her or not.

She was sleeping peacefully in her little crystal cradle, hugging Snuggles, her favourite teddy bear. She must have taken it with her when nasty Grandma stole her from BallyBoo.

"Look, Sheepig, I've found my little sister!" said Luan in delight as Sheepig landed at the top of the stairs, panting all the way.

"My word, my boy, I'm not surprised you travelled half way across the world to rescue such a beautiful little lady", he remarked, studying the sleeping child closely.

Luan was never so happy to see anyone in his entire life as he was to see Seersha right now. Wait until he brought her back to his mum! He bundled her up in his bleeding arms, and tried to hide her under his black fairy wig.

Cara still hadn't whistled so he must be o.k. for time. He scanned the shelves and shelves of sparkling crystal-covered books decoring the walls, hoping to see *The Glorious Book of Change* amongst them. But he didn't. He scanned the entire room.

No luck.

He simply *had* to find it.

"Where's *The Glorious Book of Change*, Seersha?" he asked but she was still sound asleep.

Cara's whistle pierced the morning sky. It was time to go before nasty Grandma caught them. She must be up out of bed already.

He took one last desperate look round. He would just have to come back to find it some other time ...

They jumped out of their skins. A voice like none other boomed through the sky, so powerful that it rocked the very foundations of the Crystal Tower of Light. Sheepig and Luan looked at each other in terror. Even though they had never heard that voice before, it unmistakably belonged to Queen Danu the Great. And she was in the building. There was no way of escape.

"What will we do, Sheepig - there's no way out - there's no-one to save us - there will be hundreds of soldiers lying in wait for us!" said Luan, growing more hysterical by the second. Seersha woke up and started to cry with all the commotion.

"Sssh!" said Sheepig, "doesn't the baby understand me when I tell her to shut up, my boy? Honestly, the children of today...why, when I was a sheepiglet back in the Sty ..."

"We don't have time for stories, Sheepig, we've got to get out of here and quick!" said Luan in a panic.

"Alright, alright, my boy", Sheepig muttered crossly, "if it makes you happy". Seersha stopped crying again, exhausted by all the effort it was taking. They could hear slow, heavy footsteps on the stairs.

"Queen Danu is marching up the steps", Sheepig announced perfectly calmly, confirming Luan's suspicions. "She knows you're here. She's thinking terrible, evil, cruel thoughts about what she's going to do with you once she digs her claws into you, my boy. I dare say I shouldn't reveal those thoughts to you just yet - not while a glimmer of hope remains".

"Glimmer of hope?!" exclaimed Luan, "did you hear that, Seersha? I think Sheepig has finally gone mad!"

"Have you forgotten, Mr Luan, that you can hide yourself and your sister from even the greatest fairy eye by the gift of magical mist? And that includes Queen Danu the Great herself", Sheepig snapped, disgusted that Luan would even suggest that he had gone mad. Luan had indeed forgotten his magical gift in his panic.

Queen Danu's footsteps drew closer, growing louder and louder.

"When Queen Danu arrives, I'm going to pretend to be you, and you, my boy, are going to use your magical mist to race out of this fort faster than you've ever raced before, and bring that little sister of yours back to where you both belong".

Sheepig pulled Luan's wig off his head and fixed it hurriedly onto his own. "You're mad!" Luan repeated, "Nasty Grandma knows perfectly well that I'm a human boy and not a Sheepi ..."

"Vell, vell, vell, vat do ve have here?"

Sheepig and Luan had been too busy arguing to notice Queen Danu the Great's entrance behind them. They were shocked by her appearance. How could such a woman possibly be related to Luan? How could she possibly be his mother's mother?

Luan shoved his thumb into his mouth and imagined he was invisible as quickly as he could. He hoped against hope that nasty Grandma hadn't spotted him with Seersha in his arms. It worked, or so he thought. A steaming wispy mist covered the brother and sister from sight, and nasty Grandma walked right through them.

Luan could still see everything around him despite the mist, such was the power of his magical gift. He felt his blood run cold as he watched nasty Grandma's every move. He had expected her to look like a mixture between the clairy and Warty the teacher. Instead she was the most stunningly graceful woman he had ever seen. Her hair was pure white, like flowing strands of silk. It trailed like a veil as she moved. Her lips were pure cherry red and her skin was pale and even more youthful than Luan's.

But her eyes told a different story. They weren't any one colour at all. They were ice eyes with irises that flickered from white to yellow to red to purple to black within a fraction of a second. They were just empty and cold and cruel and ruthless, with not so much as a hint of love within them. Sheepig couldn't take his eyes off her either. She was addictive. He stared and stared, rooted to the spot.

Suddenly Sheepig snapped out of his daze and cleared his throat, stepping forward bravely to greet her. "I'm Luana Shee, my dear, I was just sleepwalking from Child Army Camp and found myself here when I woke ..."

Queen Danu the Great tossed her head back. A laugh so powerful burst forth from her chest that the Crystal Tower began to tremble and sway from side to side. Sheepig grabbed on to Seersha's crystal cradle so that he wouldn't fall over. He was relieved that Queen Danu seemed to have a sense of humour.

"Vat do you take me for, you animal! I know an ugly Sheepig in a vig ven I see one!" Her icy cold voice sent a shiver down their spines. It was just as empty of passion as her eyes were.

She advanced towards Sheepig as he backed into a corner, knowing his life was in terrible danger. She pulled off her silk gloves and stretched out her fingers one by one, ready to wring this imposter by the neck and squeeze every last drop of blood out of him with intense pleasure. This was Luan's one and only chance to escape, while her back was turned to him. He wanted so badly to stay and help save Sheepig. But he was left with no choice. He *had* to bring Seersha home and he *had* to go right now.

"Stay vere you are, Luan Shee!" she thundered the very second that Luan turned to make his escape. Seersha started to howl with fright. Luan's face was drained of anything that remotely resembled colour.

Queen Danu the Great swirled round to face her grandson. She strode slowly towards him, making him back into a corner. Sheepig was choking and spluttering between her icy fingers, but neither she nor Luan were paying attention.

"Vat kind of an idiot human boy thinks he can fool Queen Danu the Great vith amateur magic?" she snarled, as she closed in on him. Her eyes flickered faster and faster in front of Luan's face until he suddenly realized what she was doing - she was trying to hypnotise him.

"Leave me alone!" he screeched as bravely as he could under the circumstances. His words echoed like a pathetic frightened cry around the room and his magical mist evaporated into thin air.

Queen Danu tossed her head back and laughed her deep rumbling laugh once more. "Vould you like to spend some time vith your human father in my vaults?" she taunted him, breathing icy air in his face.

Luan couldn't have answered her even if he had wanted to. He couldn't move a single muscle in his face. Her icy breath had frozen everything from his eyelids to the tiny poker-straight hairs emerging from his goosebumps.

"Vell, vould you like to spend some time vith your human father in my vaults?" she taunted once more, enjoying the suffering she was inflicting on Luan.

Maybe Luan's father was still alive in her vaults - nothing in the world would make Luan happier than to see his father again. But *she* knew that only too well. Maybe his father *wasn't* alive at all *or* in her vaults, *maybe* she was just trying to play cruel tricks and mind games with him, but he had to try his best not to give in to her magical powers, despite having a frozen face. Something was tingling deep down in Luan's body. It kept on tingling as she spoke. The tingling sensation grew stronger and stronger until it seized him and took over his entire body. He had no control over his actions. Was it something she was doing to weaken him?

Luan's body started to twist and jerk and before he knew it he was shining his father's shaving mirror in nasty Grandma's face. She shrieked a loud piercing shriek of terror at first. Then she fell to her knees and a hole of darkness pierced her body, sending it into convulsions. Her skin aged a hundred years within seconds and she turned into the wizened old witch that she was. Utter blackness poured forth from the hole of darkness in her body, crashing against the little shaving mirror and breaking it in two. Luan instantly regained control of his face and body and didn't wait in his nasty Grandma's company for another second.

Luan slid down the crystal banister of the staircase like he had never slid before. It was a one-way rollercoaster that no-one had control over. His frilly dress blew up in his face like some kind of parachute, as he prepared for their landing by protecting Seersha's head with his hands.

Bump!

He got a knock on his head to add to his injuries.

Cara was sitting on Lightning under Olkas's sprawling feet. The monster's snoring sounded like a hurricane howling through the tower. Luan looked around the crystal floor, hoping to pay his last respects to the lifeless Ziphump before he left. But Ziphump had vanished from sight. He didn't have time to look for the camel's body, he *had* to keep on going before nasty Grandma realized that Seersha was gone.

"Come on! She'll come looking for you soon! Come on, quick, Luan! Come on, before she murders us!" whispered Cara in a strained voice, petrified at what could happen if they didn't leave there and then.

Luan picked himself up and slung himself and Seersha onto the white horse behind Cara Shee.

Thumb in mouth, his cloud of magical mist engulfed them all. And they were off like a shot, relying on the arrow of his home-detector to guide them safely back to where they belonged. He didn't see the fort as they left. They just whizzed through it so fast that all he could make out was the sparkling brightness of it all. He felt like a plane speeding across the sky. They swept past Queen Danu's guards who had since woken up, bowling them over like skittles. The guards were totally baffled. What was that mist that had knocked them over? How come they hadn't seen it coming? They fired shots of crystal bullets from their rifles, but it was too late for them to hurt the rescue mission party; they were long gone.

Queen Danu the Great lay on the floor of the Crystal Tower of Light shocked, breathless and weakened. But with the mirror now broken, her powers quickly increased, until within minutes she had resumed her full strength, but not soon enough to capture Luan and Seersha Shee. Sheepig was just about to trot down the staircase when she grabbed hold of him with her claws once again. She had him right where she wanted him. She had no intention of showing him any mercy. She whipped off his wig and curled her long icy fingers around his neck once more.

"Seize him! Beat him! Crush him!" she roared to an army of her soldiers who had just arrived at the top of the Crystal Tower of Light. She cast the wriggling Sheepig into their midst, saying, "Make the ugly Sheepig suffer, feed him to my vater snakes in the vaults!"

"No, no, please don't!" cried Sheepig in horror, but it was too late. Queen Danu the Great walked slowly over to Seersha's cradle and stared into it, letting the reality of what had just happened sink in. Her eyes turned icier than ever before. Her granddaughter wasn't there. Seersha Shee was gone. Luan Shee was gone. Luan Shee had managed to overcome Queen Danu the Great, the most powerful fairy ever to live. He was going to pay for this.

Home
Sweet
Home

13

Every single person in Teernoman, from the dwairies and clairies to the fairies of Ice Town, covered their ears when Queen Danu let out her deafening wail of rage. All the crystal in the Tower of Light shattered, breaking into tiny little pieces with the power of her almighty wail, and the sun shuddered above it. A blizzard of crystal swept onto the ground, spattering over the entire crystal palace of Teernoman. The volcanoes rumbled and trembled from deep within, spilling a sticky coat of lava over their sides. Luan and Cara heard the almighty wail too, as Lightning bolted across the foaming sea, on its journey back to BallyBoo.

Queen Danu the Great was hysterical. She had been tricked. Luan Shee and this pretentious Sheepig animal had tricked *her*, Queen Danu the Great, the most powerful fairy ever to live. She couldn't let them away with it. She wouldn't. How *dare* they steal her granddaughter from her.

It was time for revenge.

"Fairy armies of Teernoman!" she boomed from the top of the remains of the Tower of Light, while pieces of crystal snowed down on top of the rest of her fort. Her fairy armies gathered together in front of her.

"Princess Seersha has been stolen by a vicked human traitor. I forbid each and every vone of you to eat, drink or sleep until you have found my granddaughter and killed Luan Shee!" she screeched, as her veins almost popped out of her neck in rage. "And voever kills Luan Shee shall receive a reward of vone million diamonds!"

"Never forget that Queen Danu the Great sees all. Queen Danu the Great hears all and Queen Danu the Great punishes all vo betray her! Now go!" she screeched, casting her icy hands high into the air with anger.

Her armies marched swiftly through her fairy fort and all across Teernoman, searching for any trace of Luan or princess Seersha. They searched high and low, leaving no stone unturned. They spread out and sniffed out the human scent in Buttercup Glen and in the rubble of the Clairy's Den, but the scent was stale and days old. They arrived at the coast where Dwaireen Dwairy had been arrested, and lost the scent. The sea breeze had blown it away.

They couldn't possibly go back to Queen Danu the Great empty handed. She would skin them alive. No, they cast their eyes out to the vast ocean, and launched a fleet of a thousand crystal fairy ships to sail to BallyBoo.

Luan was blissfully unaware that there was an entire fairy army not so far behind him. As far as he was concerned, his rescue mission had been successful, and he had saved little Seersha, just like he had planned. Just looking at her sleeping in his arms, he knew she was worth every bit of the trouble he had gone to in order to save her. He felt *terrible* about leaving Sheepig all on his own with nasty Grandma though, especially when he had made a deal to help him return to the Sty. For such a cowardly animal, he had turned out to be incredibly brave! And he felt *even more* terrible about the fate of poor Ziphump. But right now, he had no choice but to bring Seersha home safely. Maybe then he could return to Teernoman to find *The Glorious Book of Change*. Maybe he could use the magic from *that* book to restore the sun to Ice Town and save Sheepig and help him return home to the Sty, like he had agreed he would. After all, a deal was a deal.

Cara knew that Queen Danu would have sent an army to find them, and find them they *would* sooner or later, magical mist or no magical mist.

"Faster, faster, Lightning!" she whispered in Lightning's ear, and Lightning bolted across the sea faster than the speed of light. He kicked his hind legs through the surface of the waves, sending fountains of gushing spray high into the air behind them.

Anna Shee was looking absently through the little window of her cottage. Dawn had just broken but she hadn't got a wink of sleep.

She watched the tide rising, slowly at first, but then she watched it rise high with fury. She listened to the sea breeze rustling through the long wild grasses lining the village boundaries and then she listened to it as it turned into mighty bellowing gusts of wind, thrusting the hungry waves forward to chomp and gargle the coastline in massive gulps, before spitting it out again. Torrents of rain began to pound down on the roof of her little cottage. Something had happened out at sea to make the weather change so dramatically. There was only one thing that could cause such a drastic change - magical power emanating from Teernoman, she was sure of it.

Anna thought she saw something moving towards the shore through the corner of her powerful eye. It was hard to tell through the churning, choppy sea and ceaseless rainfall. What Anna could see certainly wasn't a fisherman's boat because it was too blustery and no sane person ever went out in a boat in those hazardous conditions if they wanted to come back alive! Well what was it then?

Anna ran out of her cottage, struggling against the wind to shut the front door behind her, before the wind tore it off its hinges altogether and swallowed it into the belly of the storm. She clambered down to the shore, almost choking herself as her hair tangled and wrapped itself around her neck. She was watching her glimmer of hope as it grew bigger and bigger all the time. It was a mist, a magical mist from Teernoman - she could smell it on the wind!

And wait, hold on, the mist was gone, and there was a great white horse in its place and there was Luan on the horse and Cara Shee and that must be Seersha cradled firmly between Luan's arms!

Anna Shee couldn't believe her stinging, watering eyes. It was too much to take in. For weeks and weeks she had dreamed of seeing her children again, but those were only dreams and she never expected them to come true! And to top it all, her best friend Cara Shee was with her children!

Anna went weak at the knees. She just couldn't believe what was happening.

"Luan! Seersha! Cara!" she screamed in ecstasy, as she waded into the ferocious icy sea to welcome them home. Her voice was drowned out by the howling wind and waves crashing against the shore.

"I can't believe you've made it home!"

Luan could see the figure of his mother in front of him. He didn't say a word. He couldn't. He had a lump in his throat on seeing his mother again. A lump so big that he was afraid he would choke on it. He just lunged towards her and hugged and hugged her and wouldn't let go of her in case the wind would blow him away from her forever this time.

Anna hauled the weary travellers back to the shelter and safety of their little cottage where she set a crackling fire blazing in the hearth to welcome them home.

"My, how you've grown and look at the state of those awful cuts all over your body, Luan! And where has your beauty-spot gone?" she gasped, seeing the boy through the dancing, flickering firelight for the first time.

"You've no idea, mum!" laughed the exhausted Luan as he pulled off his home-detector which was burning him like a red-hot poker, and telling her his tale of being stretched by Sheepig and the Clairy, while she healed his skin with the touch of her soothing magical hand. Then he went on to tell tale after tale of his great adventure in Teernoman until he very nearly lost his voice from talking too much.

"Nasty Grandma said that dad is a prisoner in her vaults, even though I think she might be lying", Luan had piped up as soon as he had found his voice.

On hearing that, Anna couldn't focus on any of Luan's other stories. Her head was spinning and her heart was thumping. She had always accepted that her husband was dead, since he had disappeared off the face of the earth without a trace; but now she wasn't so sure. If there was even the tiniest possibility that her beloved husband was being held prisoner in nasty Grandma's vaults, nothing was going to stop her from going home to Teernoman herself to save him, now that her children were safe once more.

"Mum!" said Luan, realising she wasn't listening to him.

"Mum!"

"Sorry dear, what is it?" asked Anna, momentarily snapping out of her daze.

"There's one thing I can't work out. How come dad's shaving mirror was so magical that it nearly killed nasty Grandma?"

"What have I always told you about mirrors, Luan?"

He rattled another of his mother's phrases off by heart.

"They reflect the soul and always tell the truth whether we like it or not". But despite being able to repeat his mother's wise saying effortlessly, he had never really understood it.

"Exactly, my dear! The magic of a mirror is that it always reveals the truth. Nasty Grandma doesn't have a soul, and she can't bear to see the truth about herself - that she's cold and empty and heartless. Truth weakens her like nothing else can, that's why there isn't a single mirror in Teernoman. Does that make sense?" Luan nodded sleepily. He was beyond exhaustion at this point.

Anna tucked a blanket around Luan to keep him warm, and kissed him good night. He was holding something close to his heart. Anna had a peek.

"My locket of remembrance! I was wondering where that had got to!" she said, feeling happy for the first time in as long as she could remember. It felt so good to have her children back home again, even if she wasn't going to be with them for long.

She kissed Seersha too, just as the child dozed off again. The little girl was so tired that she barely opened an eye all night.

Cara Shee had been sitting quietly, warming herself by the fireside while Luan told his tales. As the seconds and minutes ticked by, the flickering firelight cast shadows upon her, hiding her quickly ageing skin from sight. Soon she had lost her youthful appearance thanks to her arrival on human soil, and the early signs of wrinkles began to take shape upon her still pretty face. But that wasn't what was worrying Cara Shee. Suddenly, she began to speak.

"Things are bad in Teernoman, Anna; things are terrible in fact. We need you to come home and save us from your mother's reign of terror. You're the only one who can do it".

"I know, Cara, I shall return, especially if my husband is a prisoner there like my mother told Luan, but we can't go to Teernoman this second. I have to find somewhere safe to send my children first".

"You're right! Your mother knows that Luan has stolen Seersha from her, and judging by the sudden change of weather I'm quite sure there's a fairy army on its way here right now, a fairy army looking for war", said Cara, shaking her head sadly.

"I thought as much", Anna replied quietly. "I wouldn't like to see the look on the faces of the people of BallyBoo when all the crystal fairy ships arrive!" she chuckled quietly, despite the gravity of the situation.

"How fast can your horse move?" she asked in a more serious tone.

"Lightning? He can travel even faster than the speed of light!"

"Good", said Anna, "we're going to need him! Here, will you give me a hand to pack my bags?"

Anna and Cara quickly began to stuff everything that Anna and Luan and Seersha had ever owned into a giant rucksack while the children slept. They mounted Lightning with the children safely tucked under their arms, along with Spike the dog, who was snoozing without a care in the world. They sped off without a trace, to a faraway place where they hoped Queen Danu the Great's army would never find them. They hoped that they could get settled into a new life, a new life in a place where the people were so much nicer than the people of BallyBoo.

But unfortunately for the Shee family, nasty Grandma was never going to give up on getting her revenge on them, nor was she going to give up on her wish to steal Seersha back. As long as she lived, there was always going to be trouble lurking round the corner for the Shees, no matter where they tried to hide. Anna Shee knew only too well that her destiny had a cruel habit of catching up with her, and now, more than ever, she would have to battle against it, for the sake of her children and husband and all the good fairies of Teernoman. But could she succeed? Would she succeed? Only time would tell.

Glossary

Several of the names given to people in this story have been derived from Gaelic words

Anna is the **mother of all other Gods** in Gaelic mythology.

Cara is the Gaelic word for **"friend"**

Danu is the name of a mythical **Gaelic goddess of wealth**

Eerlish, spelt *"Iarlais"* in Gaelic means **"changeling"**. A changeling is a creature from the fairyworld, which is left in the place of a human baby who has been stolen

Luan comes from the mythological Gaelic name *"Lug"* meaning **"light"**, **"brightness"** and **"master of all the arts"**

Olkas, spelt *"Olcas"* is the Gaelic word for **"badness"** or **"evil"**

Piansa Toun, spelt *"Pian sa Tóin"* is the Gaelic phrase for **"pain in the bum"**!

Seersha, spelt *"Saoirse"* is the Gaelic word for **"freedom"**

Shee, spelt *"Sí"* is the Gaelic word for **"fairy"**

Teernoman, spelt *"Tír na mban"* means **"The Land of Women"** in the Gaelic language